Wolf

Curse of the Hybrids

Book 3

LISA LAGALY

PUBLISHING

Published in the United States of America

First Printing, 2025

ISBN
ebook: **978-1-966455-08-0**
paperback: **978-1-966455-09-7**

LL Publishing
Lisa1.author@gmail.com

Dedicated

To my   firstborn
Adventurer, experimenter, creator.
Fixer,   helper,   inspiration.
You have soared faster and farther
Than I ever envisioned.
I (heart) U

1

Honey

"There she is!" Luca opened the door and gestured grandly toward the room behind him. "Come in, come in. Your pizza is already here and waiting. We even have a plate and a seat for you so you don't have to sit under the table."

"Very funny," Honey said. Her face felt like it would split, her grin was so big. Luca pulled her into a tight, exuberant hug. She'd seen the guys a couple of times over winter break, but she'd missed having them around all the time along with the school and her witch friends. Her packmates were nice enough *now* but the guys had always had her back.

"I missed you," Luca said into her shoulder.

"We just saw her two hours ago," Nathan said, tugging Honey away from Luca and giving her his own, less suffocating hug. Across the living/kitchen area of her friends' dorm suite, Liam gave her a two-finger wave from the counter where he was preparing himself a plate.

"Is Charlize coming?" she asked Liam over Nathan's shoulder.

"No. She wanted to finish organizing and decorating her room before classes start tomorrow."

"Decorate?" Honey asked, wondering which holiday she was forgetting.

"It means to clutter up a room with theme- or holiday-based doodads," Walter said just before he pulled her into his arms and tucked her under his chin. She snuggled closer to his flannel shirt and took a deep breath. Of her four friends, Walter always smelled the best – like her favorite laundry detergent.

After Walter released her, she grabbed a plate and a couple of pieces of pizza from 'her' box then plopped onto the couch between Luca and Walter where they'd saved her a seat. "What are we watching?"

"Sherlock Holmes," Nathan informed her from the chair at the end of the coffee table.

"Did Liam pick it out?" Honey asked.

"No, the birthday boy did."

"Excellent." She patted Walter's knee. Other than that weird country movie they'd started but never finished, Walter had good taste. "What did you get for your birthday?"

"His grandma got him a suit," Luca volunteered. "It's green. It goes well with his car. If we were living in the 70's he'd be quite fashionable."

"My car is only fifteen years old, and the suit is brand new," Walter stated calmly.

"Just because no one else was ever fashion-blind enough to wear it doesn't make it brand new," Luca argued.

Outside in the hall there was a thump, then a string of loud, made-up obscenities. A second male voice responded in kind, but his tone was all in fun.

Luca let out an exasperated sigh and shook his head. "Immature brats. We should get an apartment."

Honey elbowed him. "Didn't you do the same thing earlier when you tripped over your own feet and blamed it on Nathan?"

"It wasn't my feet; it was the strap on my bag."

"Right."

"What classes do you have tomorrow, Honey?" Walter asked.

"Calculus II, Chemistry II, and Psychology. What do you have?"

"Elementary Engineering Design, Calculus II, and Chemistry II, but not the same ones as you unless you switched."

"No."

"Did you get your license so you could ride your motorcycle to school?" Nathan inquired.

Now was the time. She still hadn't told her friends her age. She meant to, but it never came up in conversation and she felt odd just blurting it out after she'd kept it to herself so long.

She took a fortifying breath and said, "No. I have to wait another year."

"Why? Did you fail the test too many times?" Luca asked. "That happened to one of my brothers."

"This is Honey we're talking about," Nathan reminded him. He turned to her. "Why do you have to wait?"

"Because I'm only fifteen."

Walter paused mid-bite and turned his solemn gaze on her. Nathan coughed. Luca gave her a wide-eyed look, then threw his head back and laughed.

"I knew it. I knew you were a child genius," he proclaimed when he finally stopped.

"You did not."

"Well, I thought you were sixteen or seventeen, but I was close."

"No you weren't."

"You don't seem surprised," Walter said to Liam who was settling into the chair on the other end of the coffee table.

"I'm not. I knew she was younger than we thought. She's a lot like my little sister."

Honey thanked Liam with a glance. She didn't want the rest of her friends to feel slighted because she'd told Liam her age months ago and not them.

He caught her eye. "Honey, Walter told you what I was researching, right?"

All the anger and hurt she'd felt last month after her conversation with Walter about why Liam had been avoiding her came rushing back. She looked down at her pizza, no longer hungry. "Yes."

"I've been thinking, if we could prove you are different from the other hybrids, er...wilfs and wolches that have been born, then maybe we could argue the law doesn't apply."

She looked back up at him, searching his face. "You think I'm different?"

"Unless your parents lied to you about what you are, yes. I couldn't find a single mention of a hybrid who was as normal as you, if they managed to be born at all."

"How would you prove it?" Walter asked.

Liam shook his head. "I don't know. The witches must have a way to detect if someone or something has been cursed. They could tell Zavier was spelled. Maybe they could test her."

"The woman from the council could only tell *who* had cursed him," Honey stated. "I don't think she could tell what the spell did."

"You can smell spells and curses," Luca reminded her.

"Yeah, but in theory, all wolves and witches are cursed and if I'm cursed, I've always been, so I wouldn't be able to tell the difference."

"What do you mean we're all cursed?" Nathan asked.

"The curse automatically shows itself whenever a wolf and a witch get together. You don't have to touch anything or go anywhere. It's dormant until it is activated but it's there, right now."

"So, for some reason, you and your parents didn't activate it." Liam said thoughtfully.

"Maybe, or maybe my mom figured out a way to break it."

"Your mom was a healer, right?" Liam asked.

Honey nodded.

"Then she couldn't break it. She wasn't a curse breaker and there hasn't been a curse breaker seen for over a hundred years."

"True, but charms made by curse breakers still exist."

"Really?" Liam asked. "Strong enough to break a curse that affects millions of people and has lasted for hundreds of years?"

"Probably not," she conceded, "but maybe it would work for one person."

"In any event, if we could show, magically, that you are not cursed, maybe we can argue the law doesn't apply."

"I don't know," Nathan said. "I looked into the law. Positive proof of mixed blood means instant death. You can legally murder someone if they have mixed blood. Maybe though," he put his pizza down and put on his thinking face, "maybe the law could be amended to include positive proof of curse. People would argue that it's not needed, but at the same time, they couldn't argue that there's any harm in adding it."

"We're back to proving she isn't cursed," Liam said. He wiggled his eyebrows. "Good thing we know some witches. Honey, let me ask if there is a way to do that so no one has any reason to suspect you."

"Sure." She didn't need to ask. She had a whole magical library at her disposal.

The intracollegiate games were scheduled for the first Friday and weekend after classes started. To prepare, over winter break Honey and many of the other college wolves had spent at least a couple of hours in the huge pack gym every day. She'd focused on climbing ropes to build her arm strength and challenging whomever she could to fight, including some of the pack guards. They mistakenly took it easy on her at first. After she knocked one out with a well-placed kick and took down another with her Black Widow move, they got serious. Alpha Brandon even came out to watch.

Despite being in the best shape of her life, Monday morning was hard. Anyone who wasn't on a team, meaning her and Liam and about half the other wolves, ran. They did push-ups and sit-ups and chin-ups, practiced various track things like discus and shot put and javelin, none of which she was good at, then ran again. She was okay at the long jump, but until last month she'd never tried it, so there was a lot of room for improvement.

Everyone was dragging when they left the field.

She took her time in the shower trying to loosen her muscles, but still made it to her Calculus class on time. It was the same teacher at the same hour in the same room she had her first semester. To her surprise, he said hello when she walked into the room. He'd never done that before. Blaze was wrong. Giving gifts to your teachers at the end of the semester *was* a useful thing to do.

She'd signed up for the human chemistry class partially so she could be lab mates with Evie, her human friend again, and partially so she could use her powers in class to explore the molecules without worrying about any witches or wolves detecting her. This semester the lecture class was on the third floor. It was not a pleasant place to climb to after a hard workout.

She walked into the room, glad she'd found it without too much trouble and was immediately accosted by an unwelcome smell. Damien was back. She sniffed the air again, no, maybe not Damien. She didn't smell diesel fumes or that nasty cologne. Whoever it was looked up and at her like he was as surprised to see her as she was him. She wasn't buying it. He gave her a nod. She ignored him and sat near Evie who was near the front on the opposite side of the room.

It was a good thing the first lecture was only about the syllabus and a review. She was too angry to pay much attention. The anger kept building until she finally pulled out her phone and pounded out a text to Brayton. Of all her friends, and he did feel like something of a friend after all the time they'd spent in the gym together over break, he was the only one who could actually do anything against whichever Meyer creep was at the back of the room.

Brayton immediately texted back to ask where she was.

Letting off some steam, even by text, made her feel much better. She wrote back that everything was fine and that she was just letting him know.

That's when the teacher started covering participation points and stated loudly while looking in her direction that anyone with cell phones out during class would have points deducted.

Honey quickly put her phone away.

By the end of class she'd calmed down enough to smile and chat with Evie a few minutes while she waited for the crowd to clear so she could apologize to the teacher. Blaze would tease her for bothering, but Mom had taught her to be polite. Unfortunately, the wolf at the back of the room was taking his time too. Maybe she should have left.

A certain someone's scent made her stomach flip even before she saw him.

"Brayton, what are you doing here?" she asked when he walked into the room.

He was glaring toward the back corner of the room. "Protecting you."

"He didn't do anything."

"Yet." Brayton stepped between Honey and the other male who had stood when Brayton walked in and was now approaching.

"What's going on?" Evie asked, her wide eyes bouncing between the two men.

"A misunderstanding, I hope," Honey mumbled to her.

"Hi Brayton. I guess I shouldn't be surprised to see you here, not after what my brother did."

"Deacon," Brayton acknowledged. "What are you doing here?"

"Taking a class."

"Don't you already have your degree?"

"In business. I'm taking some science courses so I'll have a better understanding of what's going on in some of our pack businesses."

"And you just happened to enroll in the same class as Honey?"

"It was the class for...," he eyes flicked to Evie then back to Brayton. "It was at the right time. How was I supposed to know she was in it?" He looked over Brayton's shoulder toward Honey apologetically. "Maybe you could switch to another class. I would but it's not just my schedule I'd have to rearrange. I have people scheduled to work in my place while I'm here."

The anger she'd tamped down came roaring back. "I can't switch. I'd have to rearrange all my classes and I need this for my major."

"Oh. What are you majoring in?" he asked brightly.

"What she's doing is none of your business," Brayton interrupted. "You are the one who should switch. You already have your degree."

Deacon held his hands up. "Look, I get it. My brother can be a bit pushy. I'm not my brother. I'm not here to harm you. I'm here to learn, same as you. If it makes you

12

feel better, I'll stay in the back. You can have the front, all right?"

Unlike his brother, he wasn't swelling with alpha power to get his own way. She didn't smell any lies either.

"What's going on here?" A woman's voice interrupted.

"Just saying hello," Deacon replied before Brayton or Honey could.

"That's not what it looks like," the instructor said. "It looks like a scene from a teenage love drama. I hate teenage love dramas." Her gray eyes drilled into Honey's. "Don't turn my classroom into one."

The teacher marched out the door before Honey had a chance to apologize about the phone. Now the teacher probably thought she was one of those love-sick girls who crushed on guys all the time.

"That's not good," Evie said, her eyes on the door. "I heard she picks one student every semester to dump on. Looks like you're it."

And it was all Deacon's fault. She glared at him, although what she really wanted to do was throw him out the door and ban him from the college. "Stay away from me. Far, far away."

He took a step back like he was afraid, but he looked more amused than anything. "Whoa, angry much? Wrong time of the month perhaps?"

Warm fingers slipped into hers and Honey abruptly realized she was growling. Not enough to make Evie think she was a wolf, but enough that her friend was staring at her in concern. She'd let herself get so angry her ire was like a haze around her. She was surprised Evie couldn't smell it. Honey shook her head and turned her back on Deacon to smile at Evie.

"I'll see you in lab."

Evie looked between Honey and Deacon uncertainly, then nodded. "Okay, although," she leaned forward to whisper in Honey's ear, "I want the scoop."

"Later," Honey promised.

Brayton squeezed Honey's fingers and released her hand. She almost wished he hadn't. Not because she wanted to hold his hand, but wolves like contact. She turned to him, blinking so she wouldn't have to look at Deacon as her head swiveled. "Thanks for coming Brayton."

"Sure. Do you have another class or would you like to escort me to mine?"

"I'll escort you."

Maybe if Deacon thought she and Brayton were good friends he'd leave her alone.

"You okay Honey," Brayton asked once they were outside. "I thought I was going to have to protect Deacon from you for a little there."

She shivered. It was much cloudier and colder than before class. "Yeah. It's just, the nerve of him saying I should switch classes! And then he got me in trouble with the teacher because I texted you during class. I wouldn't have if he wasn't there. Why can't those two leave me alone?"

Brayton put his arm around her shoulders and squeezed. "Because you are something special and they can't help themselves."

"You don't seem to have a problem."

He laughed bitterly, "No, I only tried to kill you."

"It wasn't your fault."

"Yeah, but I hurt you in other ways too. I'm lucky you even talk to me."

She pulled away to look up at him. "I never thought I'd hear that coming from you. What changed?"

He shrugged.

She stepped closer as another gust of wind tore at them. Oddly, he put his arm around her again. It should have felt weird. It didn't.

2

Honey

As soon as Brayton saw some of the other pack members, he gave her another squeeze, then dropped his arm.

"See you later Brayton."

"Where are you going now?"

"That was my last class today. I'm going to the library."

"Maybe you should stay with me."

Maybe he *was* maturing. He didn't demand she stay like he would have only a few months ago, but she had plans. "No. I'll be fine. Besides, I don't want to get you in trouble with your teacher."

"Text me when you get there then."

"Yes, dad."

He shook his finger at her. "And you better be home in time for dinner young lady, or there will be consequences."

She rolled her eyes but couldn't keep the smile off her face when she turned away.

The library was more crowded than usual, at least on the lower floors, but by the time she got to the top floor, there was hardly anyone around. She fully expected the library door to have moved again, but it was still in the closet. She formed an air shield and stepped through.

There were more people inside than she'd ever seen. Most of them didn't even glance at her when she passed. She worked her way around the walkways and stairs to the librarian's office on the ground floor. The librarian – whose name was Lila Carrier according to the 'This book belongs to' stamp in the book, wasn't there. Honey wanted to return the librarian's book in person, so she started reading the titles of the books on the ground floor, knowing that would get her attention.

Like magic, which it probably was, the librarian appeared, nearly running at Honey from a door at the end of the narrow room.

Honey stepped back reflexively when the woman tried to grab her arm. The librarian didn't try again, but pointed at the door. "Go. Now. You can't be here!"

It was the most animated Honey had ever seen her.

"What's wrong?"

"Just go."

"Okay," Honey offered her the book she was carrying. "Here's your book. Thank you."

The librarian reached for the book, but a sharp, commanding female voice behind her had the librarian pushing the book toward Honey instead.

"Ms. Carrier, we don't have all day."

The librarian's shoulders sagged slightly, then she shot Honey a look that demanded she stay quiet, and resolutely turned to the people behind her, keeping her body in front of Honey's.

"I apologize. It's always a little hectic the first day of the semester. The tree is right over here."

Ms. Carrier made a shooing motion behind her back with her hand, then marched toward one of the shelves by the wall. Honey was curious, but by the way the librarian was acting, the two old women and thirty-something man must be important. She didn't want Ms. Carrier to get in trouble because of her. Besides, she could watch them from above as long as they didn't duck into a room.

"You there, what's your name?"

Honey let her foot fall and turned. She should have moved faster. A set of bright blue eyes bored into her. The old woman had to be in at least her 80's. Her short hair and the sharp way she was dressed screamed leader though, instead of granny, and she emanated power; not magical power, more like force of will. The woman with her was younger, perhaps in her 60's, and softer in hairstyle, dress, and face. She had kind eyes, but there was a general feeling of sadness around her.

Honey couldn't have said why, but she knew she did not want any of them to know her name. She gave them the name she and her mom had come up with a long time ago. It was easy to remember because it started with the same letter as her real name and said what she was trying to do, hide.

"Heidi."

"What family? What branch?"

What was she talking about? To hide her lack of knowledge, Honey threw a question back. "Who are you?"

The woman's eyes flashed and she stepped closer. She was nearly the same height as Honey and definitely the scariest old lady she'd ever met, but Honey had faced down alphas before. She lifted her chin and prepared to defend herself. Somewhere in the back of her head, three words floated by in her mom's voice: 'Honey', 'vinegar', 'flies'.

Right, the woman wasn't a wolf. It wouldn't be right to beat her up and she'd probably notice if Honey froze her. She gave the woman a deferential little nod. "I'm sorry, I didn't mean to offend. I'm just really curious who you are. You are clearly someone with great power."

Her complement worked. The woman's eyes shifted from Honey to one of the larger pictures on the wall. It was an oil painting of an older lady in a long dress that looked like a mixture of velvet and silk with long sleeves and a bustle at the back.

"I am Adelia Wixx, granddaughter of Elinor Wixx, creator of the blood and bone rejuvenation potion, and great-great-great granddaughter of First Mistress Victoria Wixx, a founder of this school."

"Oh," Honey said, finally recognizing the woman in the portrait. "That's Victoria when she was older. I saw her in the founders' photo."

The woman snapped her fingers under Honey's nose. "You do not call her by her first name! She is First Mistress Madame Wixx, Matriarch of Magic to you."

"Yes, Ma'am."

"What is your family name?" the woman asked again.

"Here it is," the librarian interrupted. She was carrying a small but realistic-looking tree about eight inches high made entirely of metal. It even had tiny little leaves.

The old woman immediately turned her attention from Honey to follow the librarian to a small, round, ornate wooden table in the middle of the room. The old lady's companions followed. Honey took advantage of their distraction and slipped toward the stairs and the shadows around it. She should just leave, but she really wanted to see what the tree was for. As quietly as she could, she went two flights up and found a spot on the balcony where the lights from the lamps didn't meet.

By the time she got there, the tree had grown big enough to shade the three people below her. No, that wasn't right. The metal tree was still the same size, but now there was a translucent version that stretched out over their heads, like a hologram.

The oldest lady touched the base of the metal tree. "Show me my granddaughter, Madeline Wixx."

A light started from the old woman's finger and shot up the middle of the trunk, then along progressively smaller and smaller branches. It finally zipped along the edges of a single leaf, leaving behind a faint golden glow.

The younger woman grabbed her chest and covered her mouth. "No."

"She's dead?" the man asked.

"I'm sorry," the librarian said with a wobble in her voice.

"Show me how she died," the older lady commanded.

The leaf turned black.

"She was murdered?" the younger of the old women gasped. "My poor baby."

"Hush Rachel," the older lady said. "Your caterwauling is not helping." She took a deep breath and let it out as a sigh that Honey could hear even from where she was hiding. "Let's try a finding spell again. Whatever she was using to hide herself might be gone now."

"Would you like to use the globe and maps," the librarian asked.

"Yes, that would be appreciated," the older lady replied firmly. She and the man followed the librarian toward her office. The other lady remained weeping under the tree.

A few minutes after they were gone, the woman reached up and touched the leaf which was glowing golden again. Honey didn't think the woman could physically touch it since it was made of light, but the woman held her finger up to it for several moments. Her lips moved but Honey couldn't tell what she said from where she stood. Suddenly, there was a little flash of light next to her mother's leaf. A glowing twig unfurled and a leaf opened right next to Honey's mother's leaf. This one glowed green.

Her grandmother – Honey was pretty sure that's who Rachel was – covered her mouth again with one hand and stuck out her arm to flap her other hand in the direction of the office, but didn't say anything for several seconds. She finally took her hand away from her mouth and yelled, "Mother! Mother, come quick!"

A few moments later the old lady stormed into view with the librarian and the man close behind her.

"Rachel, what are you, ten? Why are you yelling in the library?" the woman's mother, Honey's great-grandmother, asked.

"Look." Rachel pointed to the green leaf. "Madeline had a child and it's still alive."

The old lady moved closer to inspect it herself.

"How can that be?" the man asked.

"Surely I don't need to explain to you about the birds and the bees," the older woman snapped.

"No, I meant why haven't we seen this before? Did she just have it recently?"

Honey's great-grandmother touched the base of the tree. "Show me the information on Madeline Wixx's child.

Small lights zipped across the green leaf as it grew. Honey could tell there were now glowing letters on the leaf, but she couldn't read them.

"He or she just turned fifteen in December," the old lady read.

"There's no name?" the man asked.

"No. She must have never formally named it," the old lady said.

"Fifteen. What is that, a freshman in high school," her grandmother asked. "We need to find the child. It could be in danger."

"We don't even have a name," the eldest woman said. "We have nothing to focus the spell with."

"If the child is still in high school, there's a good chance it's close to where Madeline died. It will at least give us a place to start," the man said. "But again, why haven't we seen this before?"

"Madeline must have found a way to hide the child from the magic," Honey's great-grandmother said. "She was always a smart one. I wonder who the father is." She looked at the man. "Is it yours?"

"No. We never... I'm just as surprised as you are, but it might explain why she disappeared."

"I guess it does," the old lady said. "Did you ever suspect she was seeing someone else?"

He shook his head. "No. We didn't see each other that often. She was busy with school, and I was trying to establish myself."

"Did she ever mention anyone?"

"No."

"Hmm. Let's see if we can find Madeline, then we'll go from there."

As soon as they were out of sight, Honey raced for the exit. Even from that brief meeting she had a feeling that if her great-grandmother discovered who she was and that she was part wolf, it wouldn't be a happy ending.

3

Honey

Chemistry lab was her first class on Tuesday. There were two lab sections for the class but guess who was in hers. If Honey hadn't been sure before, now she was doubly sure the Meyer boys were targeting her, but why?

There were only four people in the room so far: Deacon, the TA, a human Honey didn't know, and herself. Just in case Deacon tried to sit next to her, Honey picked a bench in the middle back where she didn't want to sit. While she was arranging her backpack, Deacon dropped down on the stool next to her.

"We meet again," he said, all friendly-like.

"I thought you were going to stay away from me."

"You were the one who sat in the back of the room."

"So I did." She grabbed her backpack and slipped away. He stayed put. Ha. That worked. She sat at the bench in the front near the door. Evie came in a few minutes before class was supposed to start and slid into the space beside her. Deacon's eyes felt like lasers on the back on Honey's head but she pretended she'd forgotten about him. The other benches filled up fast, although no

24

one sat next to Deacon. Right before class officially started Honey caught a familiar whiff of body spray. She looked up at the same moment Brayton walked through the door studying a piece of paper in his hand.

"Brayton?"

The smile that spread across his face when he looked up and saw her made her chest feel strange.

"Ah, I found the right class."

"What are you doing here?"

"I'm taking Chem II now. I needed another science elective and this one fit my schedule."

He'd switched into the class for her.

"You didn't have to do that."

"Someone has got to keep an eye on you. Besides, I figured you could help me if I get lost."

"Sure."

He jerked his head toward the back of the room, "Looks like I get to sit next to Deacon. This should be fun."

"Watch your temper."

"Says the girl who growled at him yesterday."

He gave a two-fingered wave to Evie and casually sauntered to the back of the classroom.

Evie watched him go, then turned to Honey with questions in her eyes. "Okay, you've got two really good-looking guys drooling over you. What's going on?"

The TA stood up and clapped his hands a couple of times. "Class, let's get started."

4

Honey

Friday and the first day of the intracollegiate tourney came fast. Friday was slated for the track competition, Saturday for team sports and obstacle athletics, and Sunday for MMA. It was snowing, hard. Luckily, all the track events were scheduled to take place in the huge indoor complex in the basement of the student gym. All the competitors entered by an outside door instead of going in the main door. Honey was pretty sure that humans, and probably a lot of the witches, didn't know the basement existed since the wolves were allowed to transform there.

She'd never run on a track before yet somehow, she won the 800 and 1600-meter female races in human form. She didn't bother competing in the wolf-form races. That wasn't her strength. Liam qualified to go on to the state competition in the long jump. Greg qualified for state in the 1600-meter male human form race. There might have been a few other freshmen who made it, but most of the qualifiers were older.

The obstacle athletics course was set up in the old gym. She was scheduled to compete early on Saturday. Her witch friends hadn't been too excited about the track events, but when they heard she was doing something akin to American Ninja Warrior, they all wanted to come. It was a daring, perhaps even foolish thing for witches to show up at a wolf competition, but no one voiced their concern. Honey guessed her witch friends all thought the same way she did. Since she was the only one competing, their mutual wolf friends would be in the crowd with them if there were any problems, and the old gym didn't have room for a lot of spectators anyway.

At first, she was excited that all her friends would be there, but by Saturday morning Honey was wishing she hadn't told anyone.

She arrived at the gym an hour before she was scheduled to compete to warm up. Most of the other competitors were men, but there were a few women. They all had a lot more muscle than her, but that meant they were heavier than her, giving her an advantage, or so she told herself. Captain Young gave all the competitors a walk-through of the course about thirty minutes before the competition began. The course was heavy in arm-strength testing obstacles, but there were also things she might excel at like the bars they had to flip between. By the time Captain Young was done making sure they knew how to get through all the obstacles there were only ten minutes left.

"Oh my gosh, are those witches?" one of the girls asked. Her high-pitched feminine voice did not match her muscular physique at all. Honey guessed she was a senior.

"What are they doing here," one of the guys growled.

Honey pulled up a big grin. "They're with me. They all wanted to see how good wolves are at a course like this, so I invited them."

"You're an idiot," the girl said. "They're going to jinx you and make you fall."

"Well, if they do, you will have one less competitor."

"True, although I wasn't really counting you anyway."

Honey shrugged. She just wanted to try to make it through the course. She had no expectations of winning.

She was the third person to run the course. The other two freshman whom Captain Young thought would have a chance fell before they finished it. They could still qualify as long as everyone fell earlier in the course than they did. Honey was pretty sure that wouldn't happen.

It sounded like she had more people cheering for her than anyone else so far when she stepped up to the line. Daegal, whose spell casting was slowly getting better, made a cascade of magical sparkles shoot from his fingertip and threw her a kiss with his other hand.

The official with the starting gun growled under his breath at Daegal before turning to her. "You ready, Miss Smith?"

She took a deep breath and nodded. The first obstacle was a series of blocks she had to jump back and forth between. The first guy had taken little stutter steps after every jump, slowing him down. She'd decided to make continuous leaps and skip the stuttering. The gun went off. Her idea worked. At the end was a rope to swing to another platform. From there she jumped onto a swinging bar, released and grabbed a second one, then jumped onto a big swinging pillar before leaping to the next platform. She was already farther than the first freshman. After that was a series of bars she had to run across. They didn't even spin. Next was the first test of strength. She had to use two big hoops to climb up a slanted pole with pegs and then down another one. She'd seen something like it on TV. With a lot of body swinging, she made it through without wearing her arms out too much.

The sixteen-foot wall was next. That was easy. Then there was a series of large pipes on chains. She nearly fell backwards when she landed on the platform but managed to catch herself. Over all the people yelling, she could have sworn she heard Brayton's voice, but she didn't look back. Another test of balance, then a really, really long leap. She wasn't sure she could make it. There wasn't much room to get a good start. She was about to go for it when she remembered Liam telling her about a long jumper in the 1970's who'd used a front flip to add distance to his jump. The move was banned for safety concerns, but she wasn't landing in a hard sand pit. A thick, cushy pad awaited her. She rocked back, then ran as hard as she could in the short space. As soon as her feet left the ground, she flipped forward. She came out of the flip just in time to grab the edge of the platform and pull herself up. The gym exploded with cheers. Two more obstacles to go. Next was a horizontal climbing wall. She'd never climbed anything except a jungle gym. She tried. She got about half-way across and realized she just didn't have the strength to go any farther. She didn't want to fail, but there wasn't anything else she could do. She let go.

Instead of water like on TV, there was a big thick mat beneath her. She laid on it for a few moments, then rolled off. The next competitor was already stepping up to the line. Captain Young patted her on the back. "You almost made it. I am impressed. That was a great jump."

Her friends surrounded her when she stepped past the rope barrier and patted and congratulated her even though she'd failed. Luca had her whole attempt on video. She couldn't tell if the flip helped with the jump. It did look cool though.

The two people after her didn't make the jump, but they were sophomores. She left after that to go to Walter's basketball game.

On Sunday, all the freshmen were required to compete in the MMA portion. Captain Young had encouraged them to get there early, but Honey wasn't scheduled to start until 10 a.m. so she went to church first. After she got back, she met up with Daegal, Blaze, Sabine, and Panas, her witch friends who had decided they wanted to watch the fighting too and walked with them to the student gym.

The closer they got to the semi-secret entrance to the big basement, the dirtier the looks they received.

"I don't know if we should be doing this," Blaze said when they were nearly there.

Honey stopped and turned around to face them. "You can leave now if you want, but there's no reason you shouldn't be able to watch. This is just like when Luna Lynn went to your craft fair. You just have to smile and act like you being there is a normal thing to do and don't be afraid. They can smell fear."

"I'm afraid," Blaze admitted, "and I don't know how to control that."

If she wasn't hiding her powers from her friends and she didn't have to fight, she could trap all their scents with

30

an air shield although the wolves might then mistake them for humans. "Daegal, is there a spell you can use to mask the scent of fear?"

He thought for a bit. "No, I haven't practiced any scent-masking spells. I could try to make you invisible."

"Are you able to do more than a head now?" Sabine asked tartly.

"No," Daegal admitted.

Panas snickered. "Can you imagine if a headless girl walked into a pack of wolves."

Honey shot him a stern look.

Daegal snapped his fingers. "I've got it. I can hit you with a relaxation spell."

"I don't want to sleep," Blaze said.

"It's not that kind of relaxation. It's for when you get really stressed. I used it on myself during finals."

"And how did that turn out?" Sabine snarked.

"Good." Daegal said. "For your information, I got almost all A's."

"You cheated. You're not allowed to spell yourself during the exams," Sabine argued.

"Not during exams, just when I studied."

"Are there any side effects?" Blaze asked.

"Not really, unless you don't like smiling."

"Smiling?" Sabine said with disbelief.

"Yeah, smiling," Daegal said firmly.

"Can you remove it if something goes wrong?" Blaze asked.

"I should be able to, but it will wear off in an hour anyway."

Blaze thought for a second, then nodded. "Okay, do it."

He tapped her on the head. Honey caught the heavy scent of summer vegetation and cool lake water that reminded her of the time she had gone to a lake in the middle of summer with her parents and laid around in hammocks.

"Oh, wow," Blaze grinned. "It really does relax you."

"You look high," Sabine said.

"Not high, just happy," Blaze sang.

"Ooo, give me a shot of that," Panas demanded.

Before Honey could suggest that might not be a good idea, Daegal tapped Panas' head too.

Panas blinked, then started bouncing his head around like he was listening to a good beat. "Oh, yeah. This is nice." He gave Blaze a half-lidded look, then slipped his hand into hers. "You wanna be my girlfriend?"

She giggled. "Sure."

"I thought you said this was a relaxing spell. It looks like a love potion," Sabine said. Honey couldn't tell if she was concerned or disgusted.

Daegal scratched the back of his head. "It's not a love potion, but if there's an attraction, it might relax someone enough to act on it." He lifted his finger toward Sabine. "Do you want me to do you too?"

"No!" Honey and Sabine both said at the same time.

"Some of you need to have your wits about you," Honey continued. "I don't smell a lot of fear coming from you two like I was Blaze. You'll be fine as long as you don't try to get too cozy with the wolves."

"Oh, good point," Daegal said quickly which made Honey wonder who he was attracted to and if he was afraid his spell would make him act on it.

32

"Okay, let's do this. Let me do the talking," Honey said.

"You go, babe," Panas said.

Blaze elbowed him. "You can't call other people babe when you have a girlfriend."

"Sorry, babe. I'm new at this."

Sabine rolled her eyes. "Lead on, Honey. I'll keep the nitwits in line."

A big, burly wolf was at the door today. He stepped in front of them with his arms crossed. "You can't go in there."

"I have a fight in a half-hour."

"They don't."

"They are here to cheer me on. Spectators are allowed, right?"

"Not those kind of spectators." He glared at Honey's friends like they were holding cans of spray paint.

How could she convince him? "Is there a rule that says witches can't attend?"

"There should be."

"Meaning there isn't. I'm Luna Lynn's ward. We are working to improve relations between the witches and the wolves. These are my friends who are brave enough to attempt to conquer the divide with me. Will you please give us a chance?"

He jerked his head behind her. "Those two look high."

"Not on drugs. They took a chill spell. We wolves are scary."

"This is not a good idea. What's going to happen when you're fighting and they are all alone?"

"I'm not their only wolf friend. Our other friends are already inside. Besides, they watched me yesterday at the obstacle athletics and it turned out fine."

"The OA?" He gave her a closer look. "Luna Lynn... you're in the Mooney pack? "

"Yeah."

"Were you the girl who made that jump?"

"Yeah."

"They didn't help you did they?"

"No. Witches aren't allowed to use magic on wolves. Besides, I didn't need their help."

"She didn't," Blaze said, still grinning widely. "She was amazing all by herself. Also, there were some mean-looking wolves watching us and they would have smelled it if I tried to help her."

"Don't look at me," Sabine said. "I can only change the way things look." She touched her blond hair and a pink strip appeared.

"Fire," Panas said, flipping his palm over and sparking a blue flame.

"Spell thrower," Daegal said, "but I don't know one that could have helped her. I can give you a chill spell if you want one though."

"No." He looked them all over again. Honey grinned as big as Blaze when his eyes stopped on her. "Fine. Go in. Don't blame me if things go south."

"Thank you!" Blaze sang.

The door opened to a small landing at the top of the stairs. From there, the whole underground gym was visible. All the space within the middle of the indoor track was covered with mats marked with octagons for the MMA matches. Outside the track, the bleachers and the spaces at either end were so thick with people, the only way to get around was to walk around the track.

"Wow. That's a lot of wolves," Daegal said.

Honey grabbed his hand before he could tap his head. "No. It will be fine. Their growl is worse than their bite. I'll protect you."

"And if she can't, I'll turn their fur pink," Sabine said, wiggling her fingers.

"Come on, guys. We'll find the boys and it'll be fine."

Honey marched down the stairs half expecting them not to follow. They did though. She paused at the bottom to make sure they were all together, then pointed to her right. "Luca said they were near the long-jump pit. It's on the other side of the track from here."

People stared at them when they walked by. She saw a few nudge each other, but she pretended not to notice. They were half-way there before someone got up the nerve to approach them – three someones. Why is it wolf bullies always traveled in packs? Oh, right, stupid question. She wouldn't have stopped but they blocked her way.

The one in front puffed up, not with alphaness, but with not-so-discretely flexed muscles. "Get out of here mutt and take the witches with you."

No one had told her the rules but she was pretty sure they weren't supposed to fight anywhere but on the mats. He was just trying to intimidate her.

"Do I know you?"

He stepped closer, "If you don't move, you'll know my fist soon enough."

"First, you'd miss. Second, if you try, you'll be thrown out of college for fighting. Third, my guests are none of your business. They are students just like me and only came to watch."

"I'm not a student."

Darn. There went that defense. They could hit her all they wanted and with her friends there, if she hit back, she'd probably be the one kicked out. Freezing them was out too, for obvious reasons. What would her dad had done? Something unexpected, she was sure.

She pulled out her phone and opened the camera app.

"What are you doing?" the bully in front of her asked.

She held up a finger. "Hold that look." She handed her phone to Sabine and mouthed 'quick' to her then turned to stand beside the bully like she was posing with him. He pushed her.

"Did you get it?" she asked Sabine.

"Yep," she answered.

"Send it to BB."

"Who's BB?" the bully asked.

"A better bully than you."

Wolves were gathering on the track around them. Some looked curious, but most looked some level of angry. She had to do something. She took a step back and put up both hands to either side of her with her palms up.

"People. Wolves. Stop for a moment. Listen. Think. Some of you are curious. Some of you are angry. Some of you might even be confused. Why are there witches here, you are wondering. Imagine you didn't have the advantage of a wolf nose. Would you even know they are witches? No. That's because they are like us. They have arms and legs and hands and faces just like us. They are more like us than even closely related animals in the animal world are to each other. Looking at them, you can't tell we are different."

"Yeah I can. I would never wear my hair blue," someone snarked.

"Or pointy like that," someone else said.

"That's not the point."

"No, the point is, they shouldn't be here," the bully in front of her said.

"Why? What are you afraid of? There's four of them and at least a thousand of you."

"I'm not afraid," he scowled. "This is a wolf event. They shouldn't be here."

"Wolf event?" She looked around, more to delay and see if Brayton was coming than anything. With all the wolves surrounding them, she couldn't see much. "This looks like an MMA competition to me. I don't see a single pelt. In fact, isn't this being televised somewhere?" She had no idea if it was, she was guessing. She'd never been to a sports bar, but she'd seen some in the movies, and they always had sporting events on the TVs. "Do you shut down the bars to only wolves when this is going on?"

"What's going on here?"

A tall man with dark brown hair and light brown skin stepped through the people surrounding them and onto the track. Honey recognized him. He was an alpha or a beta but she couldn't remember his name or his pack.

He looked down at her. "Ah, Luna Lynn's little rogue. I see you're causing trouble again."

5

Brayton

Where was Honey? Her match was soon and she was usually early for everything. Brayton looked at his phone again to check the time and realized he had a message. He hadn't heard it come in over the noise of the crowd. He opened it and immediately wanted to attack someone.

"Why are you growling?" Cici asked.

He showed her the phone.

She took it from him and zoomed in to look closer. "That's here." She scanned the crowd, then pointed to where a group of wolves was gathering at the end of the track. "There."

He couldn't remember later how he got out of the bleachers. He might have leapt, but they were half-way up behind several rows of students so that couldn't be right.

He thought he was going to have to shove his way through the crowd, but they melted out of his way like he was a screaming ambulance.

"Ah, Luna Lynn's little rogue. I see you're causing trouble again," a twenty-something guy was saying. Someone's beta. The beta's face spun toward him and

38

Brayton caught a look of surprise and maybe anger before the beta's head bowed like someone had pushed it.

The look of relief on Honey's face when she spotted him caused an unexpected surge of something to shoot across his chest. Pride perhaps? Joy?

He didn't realize he was staring until she raised an eyebrow and said, "Brayton, you're puffed up like one of those dinosaur pills."

"Dinosaur pills?" What the heck was a dinosaur pill?

"Yeah, those ones you get in the grocery store and drop in water and they swell up into different dinosaurs. They're for little kids."

Loud cheering to his right reminded him where they were and he realized he was leaking alpha power worse than Damien usually did. He quickly pulled it in. "What's going on?"

"Your rogue brought witches," the beta said, looking between them with a puzzled frown. "How did you do that?"

"Do what" he asked.

"Focus your power so well. She didn't even react."

"She did, just not like a normal person."

Honey squinted her eyes at him. "Are you saying I'm abnormal?"

"A. B. Normal," he quoted the old Frankenstein movie they'd watched when her friends came for a visit during the break.

She grinned and he found himself responding in kind.

"Well, your A. B. Normal girlfriend brought witches with her."

It was only then that he noticed the four witches standing uncertainly behind Honey. Well, three of them were. The blond had her chin up like she was daring any wolves to get closer. That was bad. What was Honey thinking? Actually, he knew what she was thinking. She was trying to right a wrong she saw in the world even though no one else really cared. He should just escort them out, but with the way she was looking at him, both pleading and with that stubborn determination he'd come to know so well, he couldn't, not without making her angry with him. He much preferred it when they got along. She listened much better then.

"Yeah, her and Mom are trying to improve relations with the witches. Mom has to work with them. I'll keep an eye on them." he jerked his head toward the bleachers. "Come on."

Beta what's-his-name stepped forward like he was going to grab Brayton's arm. Brayton gave him a 'you sure you want to do that' look.

The beta pulled back his hand. "This isn't a good idea."

"Yeah, I know. It's only until she loses though."

The beta looked back at Honey with uncertainty. Brayton could see the man's thoughts running across his face. She was a rogue. It was unlikely she knew how to fight. Plus, with those big green eyes and the curly strands escaping the ponytail she'd pulled her hair into, she looked completely harmless.

He nodded and stepped back. "Okay, but if anything happens it's on your pack."

"Got it." He waved Honey and her witches forward with his hand. "Come on."

He led them through the disapproving crowd to the base of the bleachers, then up where to where most of the pack was sitting. A few of the older students gave them nasty looks, but the wolves in their class barely blinked.

Luca popped up from the seats beside their pack and rushed down the steps like an eager puppy. "There you are, Honey! Come on, I saved you guys seats."

Honey perked up beside him. "Thank you, Luca."

He winked at her. "Anything for you, my love."

Brayton barely held back a growl.

Honey threw a punch at Luca's shoulder but he was already moving away, leading the witches up to sit between the Little and Mooney packs.

Okay, he could admit he was a little jealous that Luca and Honey had such an easy relationship. Not to mention, he'd been the one to rescue her and he hadn't even gotten a thank you. His temper, which always seemed to be simmering just under the surface, was starting to boil when Honey turned to him and laid her hand on his arm.

"I didn't realize it would be so dangerous to bring them here. Thank you, Brayton."

Like magic, his temper vanished.

"You're welcome. It's all right. I'll tell the pack what I told that beta. Between us and your Little friends we'll keep them safe. Next time you want to bring witches with you, ask me first though."

She dropped her hand. "You'd just say no."

She wasn't wrong.

"Honey!" Captain Young called from the base of the bleachers. "You need to sign in. Your match will start soon."

"Okay."

Brayton could tell from the way she scanned the crowd that she had no idea how to do that.

41

He touched her shoulder and pointed down the steps. "Come on, I'll show you where to go."

The goons who had tried to stop Honey before were still by the track, but they knew better than to start something with him there. He led Honey to the opposite side of the track where two older women were handling the check-ins. The line was a lot shorter than it had been earlier.

"Congratulations, by the way," he said as they got in line.

"For what?"

"For winning the OA trials."

Honey looked at him like he'd grown a second head. "I didn't win. I didn't even finish."

"You were the only one who made the jump. They set the course up wrong, and it was five feet longer than it should have been."

"But...really?" She studied his face for a moment, then shook her head. "No, you're kidding me."

"When have I ever kidded with you?"

"Name?" the woman at the table demanded. He hadn't even noticed the person in front of them leave.

The woman found Honey's name on her list, then wrote something on a red wristband and handed it to her.

"Your first match is on mat B6 in ten minutes. If you are late, you forfeit."

"Thank you."

"Here, let me help you with that."

Brayton took her arm and tugged her toward the map of mats and out of the way of the moving crowd.

"Ever put one of these on before?" He asked as he took the wrist band from her fingers and lifted her arm.

"I have, but not by myself."

He expertly pulled the protective strip off the sticky part. Thank goodness he'd done it earlier for Cici. "For the optimal wrist band experience, the trick is to make it a little loose but not so loose it will slide off. There, see," he said, stepping back to admire his handiwork.

She twisted her wrist back and forth, then looked up at him with those mesmerizing eyes of hers. "Thank you, Brayton, it's beautiful."

It took him a moment to realize she was teasing him. "Right. Yes. Beautiful. Maybe next time I'll get you a blue one. Come on, let's find your mat."

Because there were so many people to get through, each match was only one five-minute round or until one opponent caved. They waited much longer for Honey's match to start than it took for Honey to beat the poor girl she was paired with. It was like that for most of her matches. His took a little longer, but when they finished the freshman bracket, he and Honey were on top, much to Cici's irritation. She'd made it one match below the final, then had been beaten by a girl from the Silvermane pack who trapped her in some wacky hold. The Silvermane girl never had a chance to trap Honey. Honey didn't stand still long enough to get caught.

They had an hour break while the people in the losers' bracket finished up. The crowd had thinned out, but he'd been to enough matches to know it was only temporary. The alphas would arrive soon to watch the final matches if they weren't already here.

He climbed up into the stands where Honey's witch friends were still sitting. He'd been so busy going to his matches he hadn't been up there since he'd first dropped them off. Honey was already up there with them. "You guys going to stick around?"

"Aren't the finals coming?" the blond witch asked.

"Eventually."

"You guys don't have to stay. I know being around all these wolves isn't easy," Honey said.

"Daegal just did his thing again. I'm good," the boy with green hair bobbed lazily.

"Is it safe to use that so many times in a row?" the blond witch asked the witch with pointy hair, Daegal Brayton assumed.

He shrugged. "As long as he's not driving."

"You only have one more match, right," Honey's roommate asked.

"Yeah, but not for another hour."

"I think I'll go then. I've got homework, already." She reached over the blond witch to pat Honey's leg. "You were amazing though. I might have you teach me some moves."

"I was going to get some food. I'll escort you out," Brayton volunteered.

"Heeey, that's my girl. I'll do the escorting," green guy slurred.

"What? No," Honey's roommate said, shaking her head at the green-haired guy who was sitting on her other side. "That was a mistake. I was under the influence."

He grabbed both her hands then leaned forward and puckered his lips. "But I love you."

"Are you sure that wasn't a love spell?" the blond witch asked.

"Well, I've never tried to kiss anyone when I've used it, but I was always by myself," Daegal admitted.

44

"Does that mean you kissed yourself?" Honey's roommate asked innocently.

The green-haired witch turned to Daegal rather suddenly for as strung-out as he was acting. "I'll kiss you, you pointy-haired freak."

"Okaaay," Honey said, "I think he needs to go to his room and sleep it off. Daegal, why don't you take him since you spelled him. Sabine, what do you want to do?"

"I want to see the finals, but I wouldn't mind getting something to eat and visiting the little girl's room."

Honey gave a sharp nod. "I'll go with you."

Brayton escorted them, just in case. He had Honey make sure the bathroom was empty, then guarded the door while they went in by themselves. It would have worked out great if Tuula hadn't suddenly appeared. He hadn't seen her since graduation. She looked just like he remembered from her unbelievably long lashes, the freckles across her nose and her long, wavy multi-toned brown hair. She smelled like he remembered too – a little bit like honeysuckle, but not overwhelming.

A smile cracked across her face the moment her gray-blue eyes fell on him. "Brayton! How are you? I haven't seen you in ages."

"I'm good. How are you? How's senior year?"

She stopped next to where he was leaning on the wall and looked up at him through her lashes. "It's great. I can't wait to be done though."

There was no way her lashes were real, but he was smart enough not to ask. "Have you decided where you want to go to college?"

She casually leaned against the wall next to him. "Like I'd go somewhere else. Here, of course."

"What about California? I thought you had a friend out that way." He put heavy emphasis on 'friend'. He doubted the boy she'd gushed about existed.

She shrugged. "It didn't work out."

"Sorry to hear that."

"Yeah, well, once you've dated an alpha no one else can compete."

And there it was. They'd gone on one date. One. After that, he couldn't get rid of her. She'd followed him around everywhere. He'd go to a rugby game, she was there with a towel. He'd go bowling, she was in the next lane. It was like she'd put a tracker on him. When he didn't ask her out again, she started talking about another man, probably to make him jealous. He couldn't have cared less.

The bathroom door finally opened. Honey came out first, then Sabine.

Honey gave Tuula a polite smile. "Sorry to keep you waiting. You ready to go, Brayton?"

"Is this your girlfriend?" Tuula asked, pushing off the wall when he did.

"Um, no," Honey said, looking up to him in confusion.

"You dating?" Tuula said, stepping closer to Honey.

"No."

"Good." Tuula smiled and stuck out her hand. "I'm Tuula, Brayton's ex."

He pushed Tuula's hand down. The girl was officially crazy. "You can't be an ex if we were never together."

Honey sniffed. "It doesn't smell like she's lying."

Tuula copied Honey's sniff and looked suddenly at Sabine. "You're a witch."

"Gold star to you." Sabine stepped around Honey and wrapped her arms around Brayton's. "Come on, dear. Let's get something to eat."

He was so shocked he couldn't think of any words for a moment. By then Sabine had pulled him around and Honey was pushing him from the back. They were around a corner before he thought to stop and pull his arm away.

"What was that?" he demanded of the witch.

"You're welcome."

"Welcome?!" he sputtered.

"No. You're supposed to say thank you."

"Thank you?!"

"That sounded more like a question, but I'll take it."

"Now she's going to think I'm dating a witch."

"So."

"She'll tell everyone."

"So."

"It's illegal."

"Only if we actually were dating. We aren't, are we?"

"No!"

"Exactly."

"But people will think we are."

"And we'll tell them the truth and she'll look like a fool. She was a stalker. I thought you'd appreciate the help."

"Witches and wolves can't even date?" Honey asked.

"It's strongly frowned up," he explained. "Besides, what's the point if you can't marry."

"What if you did marry. Not you two," she said when he started to protest, "I mean in general."

"Death," Brayton said at the same time Sabine said, "Curse."

"I thought that was only if a witch and a wolf had a child."

"No. It's illegal to marry a witch. The penalty is death."

"If whoever it was doesn't die from the curse first," Sabine said.

Honey's eyes sharpened the way they did when she was really focused. "Tell me more about the curse."

Sabine shrugged. "If they have a child, it will be a monster and 'death will follow in its wake'. The only way to stop the curse is to kill the child and the parents, if the child didn't already kill them."

"That's awful. Who cursed everyone?"

"I don't think it's actually a curse. It's more like a prophecy."

"That keeps coming true over and over?"

"That's what happens when you mix species."

Honey threw up her hands. "If we can have children together, we are the same species!"

"That's the thing though," Sabine said, "We can't."

6

Honey

Sabine was wrong. It wasn't a prophecy. Wolves and witches could produce children. She was living proof. Still, her parents were dead. Was that because of a curse or was it just bad luck? Then there were all those children that Liam had read about. They weren't really monsters, but they weren't right either.

"Honey, are you paying attention?"

"Yes, Captain Young."

He squinted at her through the falling snowflakes. "What did I just say then?"

"Class dismissed?"

He gave her a stern look.

"I said, I've arranged for you to train with the other OA qualifiers. They practice at 7 pm. Have you ever done any rock climbing?"

"No."

"Thought so. There's a climbing wall in the gym. I want you to devote a couple of hours to climbing each week too."

"But I have class and homework."

"The gym opens at 5 am. I'm not going to pressure you, but no freshman has ever qualified for so many unrelated sports at once. It would be even more amazing if you managed to win state in one of them. You can practice for track and MMA in the mornings. I've arranged for a former MMA champion to come in and train you and Brayton."

"Thank you."

She was going to have to adjust her schedule. School came first of course, but maybe if she studied while she ate and didn't hang out so much with the guys on the weekend, she'd have enough time to train like she needed to. It was only for a month.

Brayton met her half-way to chemistry. She wasn't sure how he found her with the snow falling so thickly. She could barely see. Deacon was standing near the entrance like he was waiting for them when they got to class. Brayton stepped forward and pulled her behind him. Deacon put his hands up like he was surrendering.

"I mean you no harm," he chuckled. "I just wanted to congratulate both of you. Very impressive that you both qualified for state. Wished I'd been there to see it."

"I was surprised your dad wasn't there," Brayton said. "He always seems to enjoy the matches."

Deacon sighed and looked at his shoes. "Damien wasn't feeling well. Dad was worried."

Wolves rarely got sick. The only things she knew that killed wolves were other wolves, old age, cancer, and rabies, in that order. "Is he better now?" She asked.

Deacon looked up and gave her a little smile. "He's fine. I think he's just been working too hard. It's nice of you to ask though."

That's when she noticed the smell. He'd either borrowed his brother's clothes or his cologne. Either way, she was very glad when he left to sit at the back of the room.

"I'm surprised they haven't closed school yet," Brayton commented after class when they emerged into a winter wonderland that was still being winterized.

"Why would they do that? Most of the students live on campus."

"A lot of the upperclassman and the teachers don't," Brayton explained. "You going back to the dorms?"

"To the library."

"Okay, see you later. Call me if you need anything."

It struck her again how different he was from the beginning of last semester while she watched him trudge away through the snow to his next class. Was niceness a side-effect of her messing with his brain?

Even though she'd never noticed any windows in the magical library, the light seemed dimmer in there just like it was in the regular library due to the heavy cloud cover and falling snow. She should focus on her homework, but she also needed answers. Was it a curse or a prophesy? Was she the reason her parents had died? Wait, if it was a curse, wouldn't that mean her genetic father would be dead and not her adopted father. Did the curse or prophesy or whatever it was even exist?

She went up a floor to the very top of the magical library where she hadn't been before and made it a quarter of the way around before the librarian showed up. The librarian tried to be sneaky, but Honey saw her reflection in the side of a brass lamp just in time.

"You're back."

"Hello to you too, Ms. Carrier," Honey said, turning around. "Did you miss me?"

If she was impressed Honey had remembered her name, she didn't show it.

"What are you looking for this time?"

"You, and I hadn't been up here before so I thought I'd take a look."

Ms. Carrier sighed. "What do you want?"

"One of my witch friends said that wolves and witches are forbidden to marry because of a curse or a prophecy. I was wondering which it was and if there is any record that either actually exists."

"Why? Are you dating a witch?"

"No, I'm a scientist. Both the wolf and witch laws are based on whatever it is. I just want to know if it's real."

"Did you bring back my book?"

Honey flipped her backpack to her chest and pulled out the book. "I did."

The librarian took it from her and inspected it under a light. Honey had been very careful not to get it dirty or damage it in any way, but the close inspection made her nervous.

The librarian glanced up suddenly. "What did you think of my book?"

"A little dry."

A 'ha' burst out of Ms. Carrier and she smiled, but only for a fleeting moment. "That's an understatement. I only bought these because I know the author and I knew how thoroughly he researched everything. He's not so good at making things palatable, unfortunately. Come on. What you're looking for is downstairs."

Honey obediently clomped behind her to the floor two floors above the ground floor. The librarian didn't say another word until they were standing in front of a shelf full of dark red, green, and blue books of different thicknesses, but all of the same height.

"You aren't the only one that's wondered about the curse." She reached up and tugged a book of medium width off the shelf. "This is a thesis someone wrote fifty years ago, but it was very well done."

She handed it to Honey. The dark cover was embossed with gold letters that said, '*The Curse of the Hybrid – a Self-Fulfilling Prophecy?*'.

"From the title it doesn't sound like the author knows either."

Ms. Carrier chuckled. "I don't think anyone truly does. Have a look though. Maybe you'll figure it out."

Honey walked around the balcony to the nearest table at the narrow end of the room and sat down under a dim lamp. After flipping through several extraneous pages, she finally reached the actual beginning of the thesis, and there it was:

The Curse of the Hybrid
Cursed be the witch and wolf who pair.
Cursed be the child of which they share.
A monster born, a beast of destruction.

Death shall follow in its wake.
Cursed be those who show compassion.
Cursed be those who pretend not to see.
Only with death can the curse be broken,
Death of the one who should not be.

She pulled out her notebook and copied the curse word-for-word, then wrote down the first few questions that came to mind.

The author started by listing the questions he was going to attempt to answer, which were exactly the same ones she had, mostly. Who wrote the curse, how long ago, and what did 'cursed' mean? Just saying someone was cursed was very vague. Did the caster want everyone to die or just stub their toe every time they went up the stairs? It was clear the child was supposed to be a destructive monster, but was that due to the curse or was it a prophesy? She could see where the author got his title.

The first chapter was a history of the curse. It had been around a long time, for nearly a thousand years based on the stories the author could find. Before that though, it was hard to say. In ancient Egypt, witches and wolves were both associated with the Pharaohs and likely worked, perhaps not side-by-side, but on the same side. In Rome, however; a mythological witch was said to use werewolf entrails for a spell. The author wondered what had happened between Ancient Egyptian and Roman times but had no answer. After that, it was pretty much all downhill.

The second chapter dealt with who had written the curse. The author didn't know that either, but he gave a nice summary of what everyone else had concluded. It was likely several witches since no single witch had enough power to curse two large groups of people for multiple generations. Some speculated it was the coven of powerful witches who survived the black death, also known as the founders. With their numbers depleted by the plague and the male witches weakened, the young female witches were easy prey for the muscular, plague-resistant wolves who tended to prefer the beautiful witch women instead of their own beastly-looking females – the authors words. To protect themselves and their progeny, the witches created the curse.

The third chapter argued it wasn't a curse, but a prophesy that was so scary, it encouraged people to act out the curse. The prophecy was very specific in that the child had to die, but since the parents and everyone associated were 'cursed', albeit non-specifically, it made sense to kill them too.

The fourth chapter addressed the birth of monsters. There had been some strange children born, but it was not always clear who the father was. Many mothers denied the involvement of a male from a different species. Somehow evidence always appeared proving, or at least providing reasonable doubt that they were lying.

The fifth and last chapter discussed how it could have been done. It was clearly a written curse, since the words were known, but no one knew what they were written on or where, unless those weren't the words at all. Someone could have just made up a poem and spread a rumor. Those who could detect such things insisted they couldn't detect any sign of a curse on anyone. Of course, if everyone was cursed and it had been around forever, how would they be able to tell?

"Learn anything?" the librarian said behind her shoulder.

Honey blinked. She felt like she'd been reading for hours. It had only been three though, according to her watch.

"A little. Are the witches who can detect curses also able to break them?"

"That's not what I expected your first question to be."

"What did you expect?"

"I figured you'd ask for evidence about the monsters being born. I have a book with pictures."

"Did they do paternity tests?"

She nodded at the book. "He raised a valid point, but generally, it's pretty obvious when a witch and a wolf are dating."

"Is it? How can you tell?"

"Well, they tend to hang out with each other more than normal."

"You mean they say hi instead of ignoring one another?"

"Among other things."

"Like?"

"I'm not getting into a discussion of the birds and bees with you. The library is closed. The whole college is closed. It's time for you to go."

"You didn't answer my question about witches who can detect curses."

"Witches who can detect curses are the same ones who can detect spells. Their talent is not to break them. Historically, there have been curse breakers, but none that I know of recently. Now will you go?"

"Yes, thank you."

Since Ms. Carrier continued to hover while Honey shoved her things back into her bag, she decided to see how many questions she could get the librarian to answer.

"If the curse is written somewhere, where would it be and if it was destroyed, would it break the curse?"

"For a curse like that to exist so long it would have to be either engraved on something that doesn't easily decay or protected by magic. In both cases, it's likely hidden. Destroying the writing will destroy the curse, but a good curse-caster usually ensures the curse will take the destroyer with it." She shooed Honey with her hands. "You're the last one here. Hurry up."

"Do you think it's somewhere in Europe?"

"I don't know. Move."

Honey looked back before she started up the stairs. "Are you going to be able to get home in the snow?"

"Don't worry about me." Ms. Carrier wiggled her fingers. "Bye. Enjoy the snow."

7

Honey

Thanks to ten inches of the fluffy white stuff, there were no classes Tuesday. She should have used the time to get ahead in her classes, but she spent a good deal of it outside having the most fun she'd ever had in her life. The wolves split themselves into two teams and played a whole-campus game of capture the flag using snowballs to defend their forts. The Mooney pack and the Little pack were on the same side. She and all her wolf friends in the other packs convinced the rest of the wolves to let the witches play. They just had to promise to only use magic on the snowballs. Honey kind of regretted that when snowballs started chasing her, thanks to Blaze, but Daegal was on her side and knew a blocking spell. Panas was on the same side as Blaze and kept melting the snowballs before they hit him or his teammates. Her team kept Panas distracted while she snuck around behind him and put a snowball down the back of his jacket. That gave her team the opening they needed to take the flag, at least for that round.

She didn't waste the whole day. The gym was open, so she went to the climbing wall in the morning and then to practice with the other OA qualifiers in the evening. The muscular girl with the high-pitched voice was there along with two buff guys and a third, very fit thirty-something guy who turned out to be the trainer. They all congratulated her, even the muscular girl whose name was Penny, and asked her lots of questions about the jump and her flip. The trainer, Sam, assessed her and declared she was very agile and fast with well-developed bodily-kinesthetic intelligence, which meant body awareness she discovered when she looked it up later, but she needed to work on her arm strength. He had her do pull-ups and leg raises, then handstand push-ups, and rope climbing. She could barely lift her arms by the time they were done.

The rest of the month passed in a blur. There was a Valentine's Day party but she had an exam to study for, so she only went long enough to snag a cupcake and some punch. Luca gave her a really nice card with a rose that popped open when she looked inside. It was sweet, but it made her feel guilty because all she had for him was a few Hershey's kisses – the same thing she gave to all her friends, including Brayton. Anyone who had to sit by smelly Deacon for a whole chemistry lab deserved it.

The state tournament was the last weekend in February. Technically, it should have been called the 'states' tournament since wolves from Kentucky, Ohio, Michigan, Illinois, and Wisconsin would be there too. This year it was being held in Indianapolis, which was convenient for their school since they didn't have far to drive, or rather, the bus drivers the school hired to take them to the sports dome and back each day didn't have to go far.

The track portion of the competition started early on Friday which meant she had to be on the bus by 6 am. It would only be her second track meet ever, but based on the first one, she knew there would be a lot of downtime between events, so she brought her books.

She was competing against the best of the best from six states so she was completely shocked when she won the 1600. Liam pulled her into a hug despite her sweat when she walked off the track. She didn't do as well in the 800. She was too cautious at the start and ended up taking third. Liam came in second in the long jump though, so he'd be going to Nationals too.

Saturday was MMA. Again, she was outside and waiting for the bus by 6 am. She didn't realize Brayton was waiting for the bus too until he plopped down next to her. Normally, she had no trouble getting up early, but apparently, two mornings in a row was too much. She woke up at the sports dome with the lovely scent of Brayton's body spray surrounding her and a firm, yet pliable and warm something under her cheek.

"Hey, you awake yet? Everyone is leaving."

She blinked and realized, to her chagrin, it was *not* a pillow under her cheek, but Brayton's shoulder. She shot up and hastily patted where she'd been sleeping, both to smooth it and to make sure there wasn't any drool.

"Sorry Brayton."

He caught her hand and looked at her with one of his stomach-twisting half-grins. Great he was laughing at her.

"Don't be. You have a really cute little snore."

She managed to turn her blush into a glare, which made him laugh out loud.

Each school sent only eight people, four girls and four boys, for MMA so there were fewer matches than at the previous meet, but there were also fewer mats and each match had three rounds this time. Whoever won would have to win five fights.

It was going to be a long day.

The bleachers were mostly empty, probably because the team sports were going on at the same time, but after the first round of fights they started filling up. Honey noticed Alpha Meyer and his boys in the stands near her team after she won her second bout. She could tell the twins apart now. Deacon was the neat one. He was always clean-shaven and his hair was nicely trimmed whereas Damien liked to sport a shadow and tousle his hair. It was more than that now. Damien looked smaller, like he had shrunk. Deacon smiled and gave her thumbs up when she walked back to her seat. Damien barely raised his eyes when his brother hit him on the shoulder and pointed her way.

Brayton jogged up to her side with a rather gruesome grin. She was pretty sure he'd just won his third match but his cheek was already swelling, there was a cut above his eye, and blood was leaking from his mouth.

"You look rough."

"You should see the other guy."

"Is that him?" She nodded to a body being carted off on a stretcher.

"Yep."

"You're bleeding."

He touched his mouth and inspected the red coating his finger as if he had no idea how it got there.

She jogged the few steps to the cart of clean towels and tossed one at him. "Sit down and I'll get you something for your face."

"It's fine." He dabbed as his mouth while searching the stands. "There's mom and dad." He lifted his hand high and waved exuberantly like a little kid.

His family was several sections down with some other pack members, but they saw him. His dad's wave was calm and very alpha-like. His mom's wave was more like Brayton's. Lynn must not have seen Brayton's fight or maybe she was too far away to see the bruising or the blood or his loopiness. Honey grabbed Brayton's elbow and pulled him to a seat. "Sit."

He plopped down, wincing a little, then grinned up at her. "Yes Ma'am".

Their coach rushed up with his hands full. He handed a water bottle to Honey, and an ice pack and a water bottle to Brayton. "Good job, Honey. Brayton, you were supposed to avoid his fists."

Brayton shrugged. "It was the only way to get close enough to land some of my own."

Coach shook his head. "Not the smartest move if you want to win this thing. You have a couple more matches."

"I'm good."

"No, it's a good thing you have a buy this round. Honey, you have a fifteen-minute break. Go to the restroom if you need to, but don't dawdle."

"Yes, Sir."

Fifteen minutes is a long time, but not when the bathroom is half-way around the complex and there's a long line. She barely made it back in time.

By the time she finished her next bout, Brayton was looking more like his surly self again. She didn't see his entire fight, but while the referee was declaring her the winner of her fourth fight she caught a glimpse of Brayton doing the same elbow to the chest thing he'd done to her when he broke her ribs. He had to fight the entire fifteen minutes and he had fresh blood on his face and a limp when he finally came off the floor. Despite how much he had to be hurting, he smiled at her with swollen lips before dropping heavily into the seat beside her. She handed him a water bottle which he immediately squirted all over his face.

The coach stepped in front of them and shook his head. "How is it that Honey looks like a fresh little flower and you, Brayton, look like a weed growing in the middle of the road that's been run over a couple of times. Oh. I know. You keep putting your face in front of people's fists!"

"I won, didn't I?"

"That match. You've got to fight that guy next." He jerked a thumb at a buff, dark-haired guy who looked much older than a senior, closer to thirty. The guy's face was flawless. "He's big, but quick and he's basically a walking muscle. You let him get a hit in and you're out."

"Sure, Coach."

Coach mumbled something under his breath and turned to her. "Honey, I think this is going to be your biggest challenge yet, literally, but if you can take her down, you're going to Nationals."

"Who?" Brayton asked.

"That girl in pink talking to the man in the orange shirt."

"That's a girl?" Brayton asked in shock. "Are you sure? She's bigger than most of the guys."

"Yep. Won-punch Wendy."

"She likes to use her fists then," Honey asked. In her experience, girls tended to use more wrestling moves than guys. She did. It wasn't that she couldn't punch, she just preferred to take her opponents down in a less painful way. Wendy turned their way. She wasn't bad looking. She had long, blond hair and a feminine face, but her muscles were as big as Brayton's. She looked like Barbie on steroids.

"Yeah, and she's got long arms. She's won most of her matches by just going all out with her punches. I've seen her use her knees a couple of times too though."

Honey had seen Wendy fight earlier while she was waiting for her own match to begin. Wendy had slammed her opponents face down onto her rising knee and then tossed the girl away like trash. The other girl didn't get up. Wendy was obviously confident she wouldn't, because she'd immediately turned her back to the girl.

"Imagine you're Spiderman fighting the hulk," coach continued.

"Black Widow," Brayton said.

"No, Spiderman," Coach corrected him. "It's going to take more than one move to defeat her. Use your speed. Don't let her get any hits in. Harass her with those kicks you're so fond of."

Coach didn't like Honey's Black Widow move. He thought it was all flash and not really useful.

When she stood to go to her match, Brayton grabbed her hand. "Black Widow her ass. Make her doubt herself."

She nodded like she was going to listen to him.

She really did plan to follow Coach's strategy, but when the girl lunged at her the moment the bout started, Honey saw the perfect opening. She did a classic Black Widow move. The girl fell hard, but she wasn't out. Honey tried to pin her, but she was so much bigger and stronger than her, she had to give up. When they were both back on our feet, Wendy attacked again, Honey dove for her feet and took her down with a scissor move, then did a Brayton on Wendy's ribs. Honey was too light to do much damage, but she did knock some breath out of the girl.

On her third attack, Honey threw a spin kick. She misjudged the girl's speed, so it wasn't very effective, but she did end up within elbow range of her face. She landed two hits with a move her dad had taught her, then planted a foot on Wendi's chest and pushed. The girl staggered back. One more spin kick and she was down, but only to her knees. Wendy shook it off and lunged at Honey. Honey front-flipped over her only to turn and find a fist flying at her face. She bent backwards to get out of the way, then decided to go all the way through with it and did a back-walkover, hitting Wendy's face with her foot, mid-walk. It wasn't hard enough to knock anyone out, but it put her in the perfect position to wrap her legs around Wendy's neck again. She pulled herself up, using Wendy's neck like it was a bar, then slung her body around Wendy's in another Widow-like move and threw herself and her opponent backwards toward the ground. Honey released the girl as soon as she felt her start to fall and did a kind of back-walkover to her feet.

Honey barely got in a breath before Wendy started rolling over to her stomach. The girl had stamina, and a very dirty mouth. Honey leapt and twisted in the air so that her knees came down just below Wendy's shoulder blades, knocking her flat again. This time, she got an arm around the girl's neck far enough to do a proper sleeper hold. It only took a few seconds for her to go limp. The referee raised Honey's arm. The background buzz she'd barely noticed during the fight was suddenly much louder. People were cheering and yelling so loud you could barely hear the announcer. She saw the grin on Brayton's bruised face just before he enveloped her in a tight hug and swung her around, giving her a nose-full of blood and sweat and him.

"That was amazing!" he said, when he finally sat her down.

"You've seen me fight before."

"Yeah, but that was…just say thanks."

"Thanks."

They heard the growl at the same time. She and Brayton turned together, but Brayton simultaneously shoved her behind him so when the fist flew at Honey's face, it hit him instead. Before she could react to his body slumping against hers, a second fist came from the other direction. Reflexively, she blocked, ducked while lowering Brayton down as gently as she could in a split second, then dove into a side-ways roll to move into a place she could defend herself against the furious fist-mill that Wendy had become. She noted pain in the arm that had taken Wendy's punch but Wendy was already upon her again. Honey didn't consciously register that Wendy's hands were low, but some part of her brain did because almost without a thought, she launched into a spin kick. Her foot landed perfectly along Wendy's jaw. Wendy's eyes closed and she fell sideways, almost perpendicular to Brayton.

It all happened so fast, it didn't look like anyone else had moved.

"You okay?" one of the officials asked finally.

She was trying and failing to blink back the tears caused by the pain in her arm. "I think I need some ice."

She automatically pulled back when he tried to touch her arm. "Ah, I see. Medic, a little help?"

One of the many people who were standing around watching several others attend to Brayton and Wendy turned instead to her.

"It's okay. I'm not going to touch you. Just let me see. Oh, yeah. That's already swelling. I'm guessing a break. We need to get you to the doctor." He pulled an instant cold pack out his kit and activated it for her. "Come over here and sit down. You can put your arm on top of it until we get everything sorted out."

He arranged a pile of towels on her lap and put the cold pack on top. Setting it down on the ice hurt more, but she knew the cold would help. She shut her eyes and imagined it healing. Unfortunately, other than freezing blood, she'd never been able to so much as seal a cut, let alone bone.

"Hey, you all right?" a deep voice inquired.

She opened her eyes and looked up and up and up and finally realized it was the guy Brayton was supposed to go against.

"Except for my arm, yeah."

"Oh, that looks bad. Mind if I sit beside you?"

"No."

67

He sat and leaned forward so his elbows were on his knees, then looked back at her. "You fought well. I don't think I've ever seen moves like that except on TV."

"Thanks."

He jerked his head in Brayton's direction. "Does your partner fight the same way?"

Did he really think she would give away Brayton's secrets? "I'm sure your coach has scoped him out already."

"He did," the guy admitted. "I was actually more curious about your partnership."

"Huh?"

"Do you practice together often?"

"We're in the same WOLF class at college if that's what you mean."

"Did they teach you those moves in class?"

"Don't they have a WOLF class at your college?" she challenged.

"Not with moves like that."

Did he really think Brayton would go Black Widow on him? She couldn't picture it, at all. "Why are you so concerned? You just won. He's going to have to forfeit."

"It wasn't *his* moves I was interested in."

He wanted to fight her?

"Honey. Oh, my goodness. Are you all right?"

"I'm okay Luna."

"Her arm looks broken to me," the guy beside her said.

"Ooo, I think you're right." Lynn looked toward her husband who was now standing over Brayton. "We better take to you both to Dr. Ziga. I'll give him a call now so he'll be ready for you. I'll be right back."

68

The guy next to her nodded toward Alpha Brandon. "Is he your alpha?"

"Yeah. Brayton is their son."

"I thought I recognized his name."

"Honey, right?" another male voice that sounded vaguely familiar asked. She had to crane her neck back again to see who it was.

"Alpha Silver?" She suddenly felt hot and cold at the same time. She had accepted that he was her bio-dad, but accepting it and meeting him again were very different things. He moved the carrier full of water bottles off the chair on her left and sat down.

"That was an impressive match, especially that kick at the end."

"Thank you."

The reminder had her looking toward Wendy. If Wendy was steroid Barbie then the buff guy hovering over her was steroid Ken.

"You used some unique moves, but one looked very familiar."

She thought she knew what he was talking about, but she still wasn't sure if it was safe to tell him anything. Did she want to tell him? Would he be mad?

"You mean the one at the beginning?" she hedged. "The Black Widow move?"

"Who?"

"She's a superhero. She's been in several movies." How could someone not know who the Black Widow was?

"Oh, *that* Black Widow."

He still had no idea who she was talking about.

"That wasn't the move I was referring to. I meant the one where you elbowed her in the face."

She started to shrug but her arm quickly reminded her that it wasn't a good idea. "It seemed like a prudent move at the time. I was too close to do much else and I didn't want her to trap me."

"You could have used your fists."

"My elbows packed a bigger punch at that angle." She smelled nervous to herself.

"Did someone teach you that move?"

"Probably."

Between the pain and all the excitement of the day and the pain, any adrenaline in her system was abruptly gone. She didn't want to talk anymore. She just wanted to lay down.

"Alpha Silver, I didn't realize you were here. How are things going?" Alpha Brandon asked.

"I'm doing well. Just thought I'd congratulate your newest pack member. She's quite impressive."

"That she is. Any news on your brother?"

Alpha Silver released a long sigh. "The remains of two bodies were found in a house fire near where Mathias' bike was found, but they were so thoroughly burned there was hardly anything left. They couldn't even guess the size or sex of the bodies."

She did not need to hear that, not when she was already fighting tears due to her arm. She covered her eyes with her good hand and hoped everyone thought the tears were due to the pain.

"What's wrong? Did I bump your arm?" The guy on her right asked.

She shook her head and asked Alpha Brandon, "How soon can we leave?"

"They're getting a golf cart for the three of you. I think that's it now." He nodded toward something she couldn't see.

"You're not going to put her on the same cart with that other girl, are you?" the guy asked.

"No. Absolutely not." Alpha Brandon looked affronted. "Do I know you?"

The dark-haired guy stuck out his hand. "Daniel Masterson of the Huron pack. My dad's a beta."

"You're from Michigan then," Alpha Brandon said. "Nice to meet you. What year in school?"

"Senior."

Alpha Brandon turned his attention to the cart that had just pulled up next to Brayton. Brayton was awake, or else Luna Lynn was having a conversation by herself.

"Hey Honey," Daniel said in a low voice near her ear. His grin fell when she turned to look at him. He reached up and wiped at the tear she could feel trickling down her cheek. "I love your name. Guess I'll see you at Nationals."

"I guess."

"It's too bad you're hurt. I would have liked to test out your moves against mine before I went back home."

"I doubt we would have had time. I was supposed to compete in the OA tomorrow." She might heal fast, but not fast enough to have a fully functioning arm in one day.

He chuckled. It was rich and low and she still don't know what he found so amusing. "You qualified for the OA too? That's impressive."

71

"That is impressive," Alpha Silver said on her other side. "Honey, I have one more question for you. Who taught you that elbow move?"

If she said 'my dad', he might figure out who she was. At the same time, she felt bad for him. It was within the realm of possibility that his brother taught secret classes, but if she said 'his brother' he'd wonder why she didn't mention him before. Ugh. She couldn't think clearly with her arm hurting so bad.

"A friend." That was safe, right?

"Did that friend have a name?"

"Yes, but I don't think it was his real one." Too much information. She should have kept it simple.

"Hey," Daniel said on her other side, "Do you have your phone? We should share numbers."

He was asking for that *now*? "No."

"Down pup," Alpha Silver said. "She's a minor, or at least she was the last time I saw her. Are you still?"

"Yes."

"What was your friend's name?"

Why did he have to be so persistent?

"Honey, are you ready?" Lynn asked.

Honey opened her eyes. She hadn't realized she'd closed them. Lynn was squatting in front of her.

"Can you stand?"

"Yeah." Her legs were working fine.

"Honey, please," Alpha Silver grabbed the elbow of her good arm but it caused her to shift her hurt one, which made it hurt worse. She winced.

He let go and put up his hands. "Sorry. I'm sorry. I'm just… I need to know what happened to my brother. If you know anything…"

72

Alphas usually gave off a smell that she'd come to associate with confidence and strength, but under that, she could smell worry and despair from Alpha Silver. There was no way he killed his brother.

"Dad. I called him dad. And he died. In a fire. I saw it. I don't know who killed him, but they killed my mother too."

There was no holding the tears back after that. Someone scooped her up and pulled her head against their chest. They were half-way to the parking lot before she'd recovered enough to realized it was Alpha Brandon.

8

Honey

Dr. Ziga had to operate to align the bones properly. They were already trying to heal, but incorrectly, which was why it was hurting so bad. There was no way she could compete on Sunday. She did go watch though. They let her ride the bus and sit with the team despite her cast.

Penny didn't outright win, but she qualified for Nationals. The coach offered to take everyone out for a celebration victory, for which Honey was grateful. She'd been wondering how she was going to get through the bus ride back without going crazy for lack of food. The popcorn the concession stand was selling wasn't nearly enough to fuel her body while it healed her arm.

Someone grabbed her good arm and pulled her into the crowd while she was following the rest of the team out the door. She jerked her arm away and turned, ready to defend herself.

"Wait Honey, can we talk? Alpha Brandon told me who your dad was. Please? I need to understand."

It was weird to have a grown man as big as Alpha Silver pleading with her. She lowered her fist. "What else did he tell you?"

"Nothing. Who was your mother? How did they meet? How could he have hidden this from his family for so long? Why did he hide it? What happened to him?"

The people around them were watching them curiously. How much could they hear? "Sure. I need to tell the team where I'm going though and I'm really, really hungry. Bad things happen when I get really, really hungry."

Alpha Silver cocked an eyebrow at her. "I'm sensing you'd like to discuss this over food."

"I'm surprised you picked up on that."

He snorted. "I may not be up on the latest movies, but I've been married long enough to know when a woman is giving me hints."

Honey wondered what his wife was like. She didn't remember meeting her on Alpha Day. Maybe she could ask over dinner. She caught up with the team and told the coach she had something she had to do for her alpha, but she'd catch up with them later, then ran back to where Alpha Silver was waiting. He drove an SUV, surprise, surprise, but his was an old Jeep SUV, not a shiny, modern one like the Mooney pack preferred. The leather seats were cracked and worn, and it had that old-car smell that reminded Honey of her mom's old car.

She hopped up into the seat and buckled her seat belt. "What year is this?"

"2000. It was my dad's, your grandfather's, if what Alpha Brandon said was true." He had his hand on the key but his head was turned toward her.

"It's true. Your brother was my dad. I didn't realize it until you showed me his picture. I knew him as Matt Smith."

"That's why you fainted."

"Yes. It was a shock to see him suddenly like that."

Alpha Silver turned the key. "You knew he was dead."

"Yes."

"You said you saw him burn."

"Yes. I came home from … well that part doesn't matter, I came home and the house was on fire. I ran inside. There was nothing I could do. They were already dead." She turned her head and looked out the window when the tears came again. This was going to be a tough meal.

"When was this?" he asked gently.

"Early August."

"What did you do then?"

"I did what my parents taught me to do if something like that ever happened. I ran. Unfortunately, or fortunately, I guess, I wasn't very good at not getting caught. Brayton found me a couple of days later and here I am."

"They expected someone to attack them," Alpha Silver stated.

"If they'd expected it, they wouldn't be dead. It was always a possibility though."

"Why?"

Should she tell him everything? Dad had said it was probably safe, but if he had truly believed that, wouldn't he have said something a long time ago?

"My mom wasn't supposed to have me. She was supposed to marry someone else."

"That was years ago though."

Honey shrugged. "There are probably other factors involved. I don't know all the details."

"You think whoever killed them was probably from your mother's old pack?"

"I don't know. Maybe."

"Why didn't Matt tell me? The pack would have helped protect you and your mom. Why did he hide you from us? It doesn't make sense."

What could she tell him that would sound feasible?

"He wasn't my biological father. I didn't know that until recently. He left me a letter. He was there when I was born. He said the moment he laid eyes on me, he wanted me as his daughter. He called himself my fated father. He also said it took two years to convince my mother to marry him. My mom was very secretive. He probably didn't tell you because he wanted to keep her happy."

"He helped a single woman birth a child and then decided he wanted to be the child's father?"

"Yes. That's what he said."

"And they were married?"

"Yes."

Alpha Silver shook his head. "Do you know who your biological father is?"

"I do now."

"Is he a member of my pack?"

She didn't want to give him too much information. He might guess the truth.

"It's not relevant to this conversation."

"It's very relevant. I'm trying to understand why my brother did this. How could he have a wife and child and keep them completely secret from our pack, from me, from my family? That's not like him at all. And he did it for what, seventeen years? How old are you anyway?"

If she told him, he'd guess everything. Would he hate her? Would he order her killed? Would he kill her himself?

"Where are we going to eat?" Her stomach chose at that moment to rumble loudly. She'd never been so glad to have her stomach rumble in her life.

He shot a glance at her arm. "Healing is making you hungry, eh? How about Italian? I know a place frequented mostly by humans so we can talk in private."

"Sounds good."

"I should have asked. How is your arm?"

"Dr. Ziga had to operate to realign the bones properly, but it's fine now."

He winced. "No wonder you are so hungry."

The restaurant was in a long, low building made of tan brick with two regular-sized doors covered by pink awnings. She'd never heard of it.

"Bet you haven't been to many places like this," Alpha Silver said while he opened the door for her. "It's family owned. Has been since the 1930s."

Inside reminded her of a classic diner with the red booths and chrome-trimmed tables. The fancy lamps hanging down from the ceiling and the polished, dark wood bar in the corner put it a step above the typical diner though.

A young-ish Italian woman, human, greeted Alpha Silver by name, except she called him Mr. Silver. She led them to a corner booth and handed Honey a menu.

"Will you have your usual, Mr. Silver?"

"Yes, please."

"And will your brother be joining us?"

"Not today."

"Oh, is he traveling again? Where to?"

"I'm not sure. It's personal this time."

"Ah. Did he go alone?"

"No," Honey said, then opened her menu without looking up.

"Do you know what you want to order, Miss?" The waitress' voice had a chill that hadn't been there before, or maybe Honey just imagined that.

"Ummm," Honey quickly scanned the menu. There were too many options. It was an Italian restaurant. Surely, they had meatballs. "Spaghetti and meatballs and a side salad?"

The waitress snagged the menu before Honey could find the dessert section. "I'll get those right out."

"Leave the menu, Selene," Alpha Silver said. "The girl just won a Karate tournament. Unfortunately, she probably won't be doing that again for a while." He nodded toward Honey's cast. "You know how hungry teenagers get though."

"Yes I do. Is she your daughter? She looks a little like you."

"Friend of the family."

She looked like him? Other than the dark hair, Honey couldn't see it.

"Why are you looking at me like that?" Alpha Silver asked once the waitress walked away.

"We don't look anything alike."

He chuckled. "She was just being polite. I want you to do something for me."

"What?"

"Look at the menu and tell me what Matt would have ordered."

It was a test. She probably would have tested her too.

"Do they have steak?"

"Yeah."

"And a chocolate shake?"

"Yeah."

"Then that's what he would order. If not that, then a hamburger. Dad might have been adventurous on his bike and in his travels, but not with his food."

Alpha Silver shook his head but his eyes were shiny with tears, so she knew she'd passed. "It is so odd to have someone call my brother dad. That's not who he was. He was a free spirit. He traveled and went to biker bars and woke up in random places."

"That was his cover. He made sure to visit us at least once a month. We'd meet him in different parks and camp or hotels and just spent the day together. Sometimes we rode dirt bikes. Sometimes we went on long runs. Some weekends he fixed things around the house. He was always teaching me things. He was a good dad – the best. I loved him. I still love him."

She put the extra-large napkin under her silverware to good use.

"Is your arm hurting you? I might have some Advil," the waitress said, sitting two glasses of ice water on the table.

"She recently lost someone dear to her," Alpha Silver replied while Honey dabbed up the last of her tears.

"Oh, sorry to hear that." The woman put a woven bowl of yeasty-smelling bread in front of them along with a plate of butter. "These are my grandmother's favorite recipe. If anything can make you feel better, these rolls can do it."

Honey took a deep sniff. "They smell really good."

"It smells even better in the kitchen." She gave Honey a little smile, then did a double take. "Wow. You have the brightest green eyes I've ever seen. Man, I cry, my face turns into a red, blotchy mess. Other girls cry, their eyes shine like jewels. It's so not fair."

She flounced off before Honey could think of a good compliment for her.

"Did your mom have green eyes?" Alpha Silver asked.

"No."

"Who was she? What was her name?"

Would he know her if she said Mindy? Probably not since he'd called her Madeline at Alpha Day.

"Mindy Smith."

"What that her maiden name?"

"She never told me."

"Where did you two live?"

"All over. We moved every couple of years, but we always stayed within range of your pack so Dad could visit. I was home schooled and Mom had an on-line craft business, so it was easy to pick up and leave."

"What about friends?" he lowered his voice, "Pack?"

"The three of us were a pack."

He shook his head. "No, I would have known. I would have felt it if my brother claimed a child. I felt it when my sister claimed hers."

"Dad never claimed me."

"Impossible."

"Ask Alpha Brandon. There was no claim on me."

"No. You would be feral. Wolves need a pack."

She grinned at him. "Do I look feral?"

"Well, when you smile like that…"

Her bio-dad had a sense of humor. She grinned for real.

"How did you learn to fight with all that moving around?"

"Dad insisted I take classes. He signed me up and paid for them."

"And that's how you learned those moves you did today?"

"That was a combination of those classes and the movies Mom and I watched once a week. I spent weeks learning the Black Widow move on my training dummy."

"Huh. Tell me more about your mom."

She talked until the food came out. Thanks to all her practice at college, she was able to avoid anything that would indicate her mom was a witch and a healer. She didn't mention her mom's degrees either, in case he remembered them.

The spaghetti and meatballs were delicious. Based on the smell from another table's order, she guessed their pizza was just as good. She was going to have to bring the guys here. They'd love it.

"You slurp your noodles like him," Alpha Silver said.

Honey wiped her chin with her well-used napkin. "I know. It drove Mom batty. She refused to eat spaghetti with us."

"She sounds like a remarkable woman. Why didn't he tell me about her? I don't understand. Did I know her?"

"That would have been before my time," she said nonchalantly while her brain kept repeating yes, yes, yes.

He gave her a sharp look. Darn. Could he sense that she was withholding something?

"Where did they meet?"

"Mmm, I'm not sure exactly." Totally true. It might not have even been on campus.

"When did they meet?"

"I don't know." Also true. She knew it within a couple of years but certainly not the month, day, or time.

"You're not telling me something."

Shoot.

"What are you not telling me?"

She very deliberately wiped her face to give herself time to think, then looked around to make sure the waitress wasn't going to surprise them, giving herself more time to think. Only then did she lean forward and very quietly say, "My parents were murdered. I don't know by whom. I think I know why, but I can't tell you. I don't think you killed them or I wouldn't be talking to you. Just let it go."

"Dammit, don't do this," he hissed. "You may only be adopted, but you're all I have left of him. I will protect you."

"Will you swear it?"

"I will."

"What if protecting me goes against a previous promise?"

"There are no previous promises that would prevent me from protecting you."

"But what if there was?"

"It's not an issue. Just tell me."

"Not now, Uncle."

She used the term to throw him off, but she knew he wasn't really her uncle, so it came out smelling like a lie. Oops.

"You're lying to me." He slammed his hand onto the table, making everything jump, including her. "Tell me the truth."

"I'm not lying. It's just weird. I've never called anyone that before."

"Still lying. Did you make this whole thing up? Why would you do that? Who put you up to it?" He grabbed her arm, her sore one, and shook it. "Is Matt still alive?"

Her bones had knitted back together, but her arm was covered in bruises and still healing. It hurt. She jerked it away. "Stop."

"Mr. Silver, can I get you anything else?" The waitress didn't sound so friendly anymore.

"Just the check, thank you."

"Are you okay?" she asked her.

"Yeah."

She looked pointedly at Honey's arm and then back up to her face. "Are you sure?"

"Yeah."

"Well, just so you know, there are cameras all over the building." The waitress jerked her thumb towards one right above her shoulder, then gave Alpha Silver a stern look. "I'll get your check."

"I'll never be able to eat here again," Alpha Silver moaned while the waitress walked away.

"I was thinking I might bring some of my friends for pizza. That should fix things."

"Honey, please, tell me the truth. Is Matt alive?"

She looked into his eyes. They were the same color as her dad's. She dropped her head. "No. I wish he was. I wish with all my heart he was, but I know what I saw. I have nightmares about it. And if, by some sliver of a chance I was wrong, he wouldn't just disappear like he has."

"You're right about that. Everything you've said has smelled of the truth except when you called me Uncle. Why is that?"

"Well, you are my uncle because Dad is dad, but you aren't my uncle because he's not my bio-dad. Like you said, I'm adopted."

"That still smells like a lie."

"It's not though."

"Tell me the truth, Honey, all of it."

From the tone of his voice and the way he filled up his side of the booth, he was trying to use his alpha power on her. She was surprised he hadn't resorted to it already.

"You have to promise not to kill me or order anyone else to do it or turn me in. Actually, just promise that if you are required to do anything about what I tell you that you pretend I never told you anything."

"Here's your check," the waitress said, looking between the both of them suspiciously.

"I swear, it's not what it sounds like. The girl has an over-active imagination," Alpha Silver said. "Here." He pulled out a billfold and took out a hundred-dollar bill. "Keep the change."

"I don't want your dirty money."

"Then how am I supposed to pay for the meal? Money is money whether it's by card or cash. If you don't want the tip, use it to buy someone a free meal."

She picked it up gingerly with two fingers. "Fine. Don't come back here again though."

"Selene, it's really not what you think."

The girl turned his back on him and walked away.

"This was one of my favorite restaurants," Alpha Silver hissed at Honey. "Get your things. Let's go."

"Maybe it would be better if she didn't see us leave together. I can call an Uber."

"I need to know the truth."

"Promise what I asked."

"Fine. I won't kill you or have you killed or turn you in."

It's not easy to break the news to someone that they're your father. She tried to just say it, but that seemed to blunt. She almost said 'Remember Madeline', but that sounded weird. She resorted to dropping clues, hoping he'd eventually figure it out.

"I was born December 13, fifteen years ago. My mom graduated from college in May earlier that year. My biological father graduated at the same time. My dad, his brother, was a Junior when my mother asked him to help her with the delivery. She was going to do it all by herself, but realized she'd need help. Do you understand now?"

His cheeks had gone an unnatural shade of white and he was gaping at her like a fish. Shock. Next came denial.

"No," he said, shaking his head. "That's impossible. I can't. We can't. We've been trying for years, my wife and I."

"Maybe it's not you."

He leaned forward. "But you're a wolf."

She used magic to stir the air around them, which also released her magical scent. "I am both."

86

His nose twitched and he gawked at her. "No. That's not possible."

"Yet here I am. Remember the first time you saw me, who you thought I was? I didn't know my mom by that name so I looked it up in the yearbook. It was her. Wixx."

"Shh." He looked around. "You're too old."

"I'm fifteen, not seventeen."

"You're in college."

"I skipped a few grades – four actually."

He nodded at her arm. "Why don't you heal yourself then?"

"That's not my talent."

Alpha Silver ran both hands through his nicely combed hair, making it stick up, but not unattractively. "How could he do this to me?"

Anger. If it was anything like the Bruce Springsteen album Dad had bought Mom, the next step was acceptance.

"He didn't do it to you to hurt you. He did it to protect you. He said you had enough to worry about."

"No. No. This can't be. You're lying to me. Why are you doing this?"

Apparently bio-dad wasn't quite through denial yet.

"I'm not lying. You can tell. I know you can."

He slammed both fists on the table and bellowed, "Tell me the truth!"

To her, it looked like he was now filling the entire bench on his side of the booth. To all the patrons in the restaurant, he probably looked like a crazed lunatic.

"Dad, calm down. Let's go before you break the table."

"What did you call me?"

He wasn't her dad. His brother was her dad, but she'd been thinking of him as her bio-dad ever since she'd read that letter. 'Bio-dad' was long and awkward to call someone to his face and her mouth must have agreed, because it shortened it. She didn't explain all that though.

"Dad."

"Oh my God."

He started crying, sobbing, actually. It wasn't an angry cry. Was this acceptance? She'd never seen a grown man cry – a truly grown man who'd been an adult for a while. She wasn't sure what she should do. Comfort him? Pretend not to notice? Everyone in the restaurant was watching by that point. Even the chefs in the back had come out to see what was going on. She scooted out from her side of the booth and into his. Unfortunately, her broken arm ended up between them, so she couldn't give him a good hug. She settled for an awkward pat on the back.

"I'm sorry." She didn't know what she was sorry for, but it seemed like the appropriate thing to say. "I won't call you that if you don't want me to."

The next thing she knew, she was engulfed in a very wet hug.

"No, no. Never think that. Oh my goodness." He lifted his face to search hers. "She kept you and raised you by herself and look at you. You're perfect. You're smart, you're talented, you're everything a parent could wish for." He pulled her into another wet hug. "And she was, she was, oh no." He lifted his head to look at her again. "She was with him, wasn't she? They were together in that fire."

"Yes," she whispered.

They were crying all over each other now. It was the epitome of like father, like daughter.

She calmed down first, probably because she'd already shed her share of tears since August. Someone had placed a big pile of napkins on the table next to them. She noticed Selene watching them, so she mouthed a 'thank you' to her before she took one for herself and handed one to Alpha Silver.

He took it, wiped his face, and then blew his nose so loud, if people weren't looking at them yet, they were now. He tossed the napkin onto his plate, then grabbed both sides of her head. She knew what was coming next.

She pulled back. "No. You can't."

"You are my daughter. I should have been there. I should have done this."

"No. Think about what I am. It's too dangerous for both me and you. People will ask questions just the way you did. Your brother knew that."

"But the Mooneys…"

"Know someone murdered them. They'll understand why you didn't claim me."

"I'll do what Zavier did then. I'll claim you as kin. If anyone asks, it's because of him. Wait. Does he know you're truly his cousin?"

"No."

She could feel him chuckling when he put his lips on her forehead.

9

Honey

The good thing about breaking her arm was that she didn't have to go to OA training in the evenings anymore although she still had special morning sessions on Tuesdays and Thursdays with the MMA coach. After a month of studying and training every spare minute, she felt like she was on vacation.

Brayton was still training with her. Even though he had forfeited the last match due to unconsciousness, Coach had argued with the judges that it was the responsibility of the officials to ensure contestants who were there and ready to fight weren't injured between matches. They agreed that Brayton could go as an alternate.

The funny thing was, she felt like she was training Brayton more than Coach was. Every time she got past his defenses, he asked her to show him what she did. He was very serious about it. It was gratifying to have someone listen to her so intently. Perhaps that was why she enjoyed herself so much even though it was Brayton. She did not teach him the Black Widow move, but then, he didn't ask.

"Honey, can I speak to you?" Walter asked when they were walking back to their dorms after WOLF class on Friday.

"Of course." She stepped off the sidewalk so they wouldn't be in anyone's way.

"It's about Zavier. I'm worried."

"Why? Does your head hurt? Does something feel wrong?"

"No. He keeps accepting people into our pack, other rogues I mean. I don't feel anything yet, but what if I can't? What if I'm too far away?"

"He's accepting other people into your pack? When did he start doing that?"

"December. I would have mentioned it, but you've been rather busy."

She ducked her head. "Sorry. I haven't been a very good friend. Where are they all staying? Is he still working for the same guy?"

Walter put his hand on her shoulder. "Honey, you've been a very good friend, you've just been busy. They're staying at the motel for now, but he's talking about getting a house. He is still working for the other pack, but he's not planning to join them anymore, at least not anytime soon."

"I'm surprised the other alpha is letting him do that. Are you okay with staying a part of his pack? Maybe you can go back to the Little pack now since he has more members."

"I don't mind being a part of his pack. He's doing a good thing. All the people he's accepted are women and children. I think the other alpha recognizes that and doesn't view him as a threat."

"Women and children?"

"Yeah. Most of them came from bad situations. He's talking about registering the pack too."

"Really?"

"Yeah. He wants to call it the Honey Pack after you. He says it feels like this is what he was meant to do."

"Oh. Wow." That's literally all she could say. Her brain was stuttering.

"Yeah. I'm worried he's going to attract some bad attention though. If anyone comes looking for those women, he's only one man."

"He's smart though. I bet he has a plan."

"He's still only one man who might be," Walter tapped his head.

She knew what they had to do. "Spring break is in a week. Let's visit him. It's 26 hours by car or two days by bus. I think car would be better because from what I read, there's a lot of driving involved when visiting Yellowstone."

"I'm not sure my car can handle that."

"Brayton has a newish SUV. I can ask him, or maybe Alpha Brandon will loan us one of the large ones the pack uses, or maybe I can ask my b…" She stopped herself just in time. She hadn't told the guys about bio-dad or that her dad was his brother. She wasn't really trying to keep it secret, she just figured if they didn't know, then they couldn't tell anyone if news came out about her. She trusted them but none of them could resist alpha power.

"Your what?"

"Alpha Silver. He claimed me as kin because of Zavier. He might loan us one." It was the truth, it was the truth. Her mantra and the breeze kept it from smelling like a lie and it wasn't a lie, not really.

"You collect alpha marks like other girls collect shoes."

"Too bad you can't see them." She envisioned a bunch of lipstick marks on her forehead. "Scratch that thought."

Walter chuckled. "You know, we could just fly."

"Plane tickets this close are going to be really expensive." She knew this because her dad had always grumped about how much tickets cost, especially at the last minute.

"Unless you have a brother who is a pilot."

"Really?"

"Yep. It would be a lot faster too. We'd have more time to go around the park. Twenty-six hours in a car? That's a long time."

"We'd have to rent a car when we get there. Do they let 19-year-olds rent cars?"

"Let me see what I can do. Car or bus will be plan B."

Walter's brother might be a pilot but he didn't have his own plane. He could have gotten them there, but it would have taken about as long as it would to drive with all the lay-overs and jobs he'd have to do in-between. They ended up using plan B, but not the way they'd envisioned. Long, convoluted story short, when Brayton asked his dad if they could borrow a larger vehicle, Luna Lynn declared no fifteen-year-old girl should be traveling cross-country with five teenage boys even if Cici was along, so they ended up taking two pack buses on a mixed-pack spring break to Yellowstone. Luna Lynn and Bernadette and two wolves from the Little Pack, one of whom was another of Walter's brothers, drove.

It took longer than it should have to get there because they kept stopping. Charlize had a list of sites that they had to see including a famous drug store in South Dakota that handed out free ice. Why they needed to see that when it was literally freezing outside, Honey couldn't fathom. Thankfully, the threat of snow cut the cross-country site-seeing short.

Zavier worked as a manager at a rustic-looking motel several miles from the east entrance of Yellowstone. The east entrance wasn't open to cars in the winter, so they were able to book all the rooms they needed. The east entrance *was* open to snow mobiles (and wolves, of course) so it wasn't that odd to have a bunch of teenagers staying in a motel in the middle of nowhere. The closest town was twenty miles away on the only road through the area. There were no stores or places to walk unless you wanted to walk a mile down the road to a Dude ranch.

Zavier was waiting for them with a huge grin when they pulled up. He had acquired a light tan and a little weight and in general, looked much better than the last time she had seen him. She wanted to get a look at his head while no one else was around, so she was the first one off the bus. She wasn't really planning on giving him a huge hug, but he threw his arms open, and she ran into them.

He spun her around and whispered, "Hey cous," into her ear before putting her back down on her feet.

"Bio-dad told you who I was?"

He laughed. "That's what you're calling him?"

"Sometimes. Nobody else knows though," she said in a low voice before turning to watch everyone else spill out of the buses.

"Gotcha." He rubbed her head, but it didn't mess up her hair because she had her warm beanie on.

He hugged Walter next, but it was a manly kind of hug that ended with a handshake. "How's my favorite beta?"

"I'm your only beta."

"True, that." Zavier took a step back and raised his hands in welcome to everyone. "Welcome to the Lost Pony Inn." He touched his chest. "I am personally very pleased that you chose to stay with us. You guys are in for a special treat. We just finished installing a brand-new hot tub. You'll be the first ones to try it out. You may want to save that though for after you ride the snow mobiles or go cross-country skiing or snow shoeing. Depending on the weather, we also give tours of the park. So, grab your gear and head inside. There's hot tea and coffee and chocolate in the lobby. The woman at the desk will assign you rooms. There's a maximum of four to a room."

It was a mad scramble for the front door. Honey wasn't sure why, it wasn't that cold outside. She had to wait for Luna Lynn to give her regards and pass on a message to Zavier from his mother before it was finally just her and Zavier and Walter outside.

"Okay. Take a look. I know that's what you're waiting for," Zavier said with a chuckle.

"I just want to make sure you're okay."

"I know. I'm sure I am though. I've never felt better."

She didn't want to stand there touching his head – that would look strange if anyone saw them – so she hugged him again instead. He hugged her back, but loosely while he chatted with Walter. He was right. His head was fine.

"See. Told you so. Now, come on. I want you to meet the rest of my pack."

He led them past the crowded lobby and up the stairs to a housekeeping cart where a woman with streaks of gray in her dark hair was stashing a spray bottle of cleaner. "This is Ruth Houston. She has two teenage kids, Jasmine and Jacob, but they're in class right now. Homeschool," he said to Honey with a nod. "It's easier and safer than putting them in public school right now."

"I am really appreciating their teachers now," the woman said. "Are you the girl who was homeschooled her whole life?"

"That's me."

"Your mother must have had the patience of a saint."

Honey liked her immediately.

Next, Zavier took them to a very warm, very humid room a short hallway away from the main lobby. A freckled woman with curly red hair was moving sheets from a large washer to a dryer while a couple of girls younger than ten but older than five colored at a table behind her. They had red hair too. Zavier introduced her as Terri Graham and the kids as Cassie and Kyra.

Finally, he took them back to the lobby. The line was nearly gone. They waited for the last few people, then Zavier stepped up to introduce them to the girl at the desk. She was young, like teenager young, but she had a baby sleeping in a car seat next to her. Honey wouldn't have known he was there if Zavier hadn't asked about him.

"Maya Fowler, this is your beta, Walter Knapp."

The girl ducked her head like she was afraid to look at him. From her scent, she truly was. "Hello Mr. Knapp."

"Maya, you can look at him. He's a good man. He won't hurt you," Zavier said softly. "Besides, he's younger than you. You can boss him around if you want to."

Maya shook her head while keeping it down as if she was terrified of the idea. "Oh, no. I could never do that."

Why was she so scared? Honey stuck out her hand. "Hi, I'm Honey. It's good to meet you."

Maya looked at her hand like it was a snake. Honey didn't take it back though. Maya eventually reached out and placed her hand in Honey's while still keeping her eyes down. Honey grabbed it, but not hard. Maya's hand was so thin and slight she was afraid she might break it. "Maya, look at me."

Maya slowly raised her head. The iris of one eye was so light it was almost white like you usually only see in wild wolves. The other was a very bright, very pale blue. Honey forgot what she was going to say. "Wow, you have the most beautiful eyes."

Maya immediately looked down again. "They're strange."

"They're different, not strange. Look at me, Maya. I want to introduce you to one of my best friends. I stole his pizza and he basically adopted me, then he volunteered to leave his pack where all his family is just to keep another one of my friends, whom he barely knew, safe."

She peeked up at her. "Are you talking about Beta Knapp?"

"Yep. He picks out the best movies for movie night, likes computers and basketball, turns into a beautiful gray wolf, and he's very smart. Also, because he's so tall, he has a high center of gravity, which makes him easy to take

97

down, but you have to be careful because he's very protective of his glasses."

"Why did you tell her that?" Walter said, sounding more amused than angry.

"Because you are."

Maya giggled and peeked at Walter through the corner of her eye. Honey guessed she liked what she saw, because she finally lifted her face to him. "Hello."

"Hello Maya."

She ducked her head again, but Honey didn't smell fear this time.

"Maya, do you have room keys for these two?"

"Oh, yes sir Alpha, I mean Mr. Brandt." When she looked up this time, it was with the confidence you expect to see from someone working at a front desk. "Honey, you're in 123. Your Luna said you wouldn't mind being with her. I hope that's all right. All the other rooms filled quickly."

"That's fine."

"Beta Knapp, you're in 233."

"Call me Walter."

"Um. I don't…"

"It's okay Maya. Call him whatever you want," Zavier said. "She came from a pack that is very formal and very strict," he explained. Once they'd moved down the hall where Maya couldn't hear them, he said in a low voice, "Her former alpha and betas took multiple wives. She hasn't said as much, but I think one of the betas forced her and when she turned up pregnant, she was given the option to marry him or be exiled. She chose exile. Ruth found her and took her in, but her alpha wouldn't accept Maya, so she left the pack."

"That was brave of her," Walter said.

"I think it had been coming for a long time. Ruth's husband died a few years ago and the alpha never liked her. She heard that the guy whose pack I was going to join had purchased this place and she has hotel experience. He put her on probation with me and she decided she liked me better."

"What about Terri?" Honey asked.

"Abusive husband. She took it until he hit one of her daughters, then she ran."

"Sounds dangerous," Walter said.

"She ran pretty far. She only stopped here because she ran out of money. I offered her a job and Ruth offered her our pack."

"Are you the alpha or is she?" Walter asked.

"I am, but only because of her," Zavier said, opening a door to a small office and gesturing for them to go in. "She has always wanted to help other women, but never had the opportunity to do so. I never wanted to start my own pack because I never saw a need. There are plenty of good packs out there. This though, a pack for women, someplace they can go to be safe, where they know they'll be safe, no one has ever done this before. This needs to be done. Your concerns are mine Walter. At some point, some brute is going to take issue with our pack and we are going to have to defend ourselves. We also need a way to support ourselves and space to grow. A motel business is nice because it's flexible, but we need to leave the rooms for the guests. Also, a place like this doesn't become available very often. The alpha I work for waited years to get this one."

He sat down behind his desk. Honey sat with Walter in the chairs in front of it. Zavier tapped on his keyboard a few times then turned the big screen on his desk to face them. A map was displayed with a rectangular-like shape outlined in the middle of it. "I've been looking into different properties. This one is the most promising. It's over 200 acres, butts up against one of the highways into the park, and is five times cheaper than anything else I can find. The original homestead is basically inaccessible on all but one side due to the surrounding cliffs, so it would be easy to defend, but there's a catch."

"What is it?" Walter asked.

"It's cursed. The moment someone buys the place, everything starts going wrong. Sometimes it's as simple as two flat tires and sometimes it's as awful as losing every cent they have. If they're stubborn, eventually they do lose every cent they have."

"Who owns it then?" Honey asked.

"A horse."

"What?" she and Walter said at the same time.

"It's the only way the bank could have some control over it without being ruined. The curse doesn't apply to animals. The last owner was the bank manager's cat. Unfortunately, the curse is smart enough to recognize that cats and horses can't possibly be managing humans, so the bank can't do anything with the land. It just sits there. Occasionally, the bank finds a sucker and make a couple of thousand, then the owner defaults and the bank get the land again. I'm very glad you're here, Honey. I know it's a long shot and I don't expect it will work, but I'd like you to take a look at the place."

"Zavier I don't think I'll be able to do anything. You should ask a witch or the witch council."

"I did. The bank has contacted them multiple times. They can't do it. The former owner of the property was a powerful witch himself. He spent years preparing the curse to ensure that the land would always be in his family. Unfortunately, he should have spent more time taking care of his property and raising children. He only had one son and his son didn't have any children. He died over 120 years ago."

"That's sad," she said.

"From all accounts, his son wasn't a very nice man."

"If it's a written curse, all you have to do is destroy the original writing," she supplied, although she doubted it would be that easy.

"It's not written anywhere. The story is that when the bank came to take the property, Mr. Witthem met them at the gate with a crow and started speaking in the devil's tongue. He then slaughtered the crow and dribbled its blood in a line all around his property. There's a cartoon of it in an old newspaper."

"There couldn't possibly be enough blood in one crow to go around 200 acres of land," Walter scoffed.

"You're right," Zavier nodded. "If he did use blood, he probably had the line mostly drawn with other animals before the bankers got there."

All Honey knew of curses was from that one book and what the librarian had told her. The part on blood curses had been short and dire.

"Blood curses are bad. The only way to break a blood curse is with more blood, but it has to be more precious than what was originally used. If it was animal blood, then you'd have to sacrifice a human and if it was human blood, you'd have to sacrifice yourself and if someone sacrificed themselves in the first place, that's pretty much unbreakable."

"Unless you can find a curse breaker," Zavier said, looking at her expectantly, "which unfortunately are very, very rare, so rare there hasn't been one in over a hundred years, or so the council told me."

She wasn't one but, "I suppose it can't hurt to look."

10

Honey

It was nearly dark by the time they arrived at the motel so they didn't venture out to explore until the next morning. Half of the group opted to rent snowmobiles and ride into the park with a guide. Most of the others rented skis. Brayton and his mom rode snowmobiles. They both tried to get her to come along but she played the 'I've never had a cousin before' card and they finally left her alone.

The cursed property was several miles away, between the hotel and the park. Zavier drove her and Walter to a pull-off area mostly protected by trees, then they all took turns transforming in the cab of the old beat-up pick-up.

Yellowstone as a wolf smelled amazing, cold and crisp and evergreen, until they popped over a little hill, and she got an unwelcome snout-full of metal mixed with unwashed human body funk. She couldn't tell if the metallic part was from the blood or because the curse was meant to shield the land. She guessed the funk was because it was supposed to keep the land in the family, but if the family smelled like that, it was no wonder they died off. After they crossed onto the land, she could still smell it, but it was faint and faded away as they moved away from the border.

It had been 120 years at least since someone had lived in the original house. She expected to see either a rotting house or a foundation. To her surprise, the house was still standing and didn't look bad. The big stone chimneys on either end were discolored with lichen, but the beams of the long, low log cabin looked solid and the metal roof was whole and rust-free. A couple of sawhorses littered the front yard, but they were water-stained and crusted with dirt. Zavier led them around the house toward some smaller buildings, pausing occasionally and looking back at Walter. Honey knew they were talking telepathically, but since she couldn't hear the conversation, she let herself get distracted by the smells and sounds her wolf senses picked up so well. Despite the snow and ice, she could hear water flowing. Curious, she followed the sound toward the cliff walls behind the cabin. Pale curls of steam rose off a small creek that smelled strongly of sulfur. A hot spring!

Large animal tracks were pressed into the mud on the other side of the creek. They looked like cow tracks, but the scent in the area didn't quite smell like cow. It must be buffalo. She'd never seen a buffalo up close. She knew Walter and Zavier would be able to find her easily in wolf form, so she leapt over the creek and followed the tracks.

She'd only gone about 200 meters when the stench of the curse increased to more than boundary levels. She followed her nose to a large pile of rocks. After walking all the way around the pile to make sure she hadn't reached the border somehow – she hadn't, the smell was isolated to the rocks – she plopped down upwind from the pile and tried to see what she was smelling. She'd fixed Zavier's curse by making the molecules in his head spin the proper direction. Maybe land curses worked the same way?

At first all she could see was air molecules floating about and bumping into each other the way they always did. Then she noticed that some of them were being pushed into pathways that seemed abnormal compared to how the rest of the were moving. She probably wouldn't have noticed if the wind was blowing, but everything was astonishingly still. She'd never tried to see what was between molecules. Could she? For several minutes she tried every method her mom had taught her to open herself up to and manipulate magic. There. It was faint, nearly invisible, but the curse was there, like the flames of a fire but cold.

Would putting out the fire break the curse? She tried freezing it first, but it wasn't a molecule. The fire was between the molecules. She could trap it within the molecules, but she couldn't hold them together forever. Could she smother it by removing all the air molecules? The cold fire immediately filled the void where the molecules had been. She should have known that wouldn't work since it wasn't really a fire. A better question was why was it on this pile of rocks and how did the flames affect people's luck? She decided to focus on the first question and let her focus sink into the pile. From the way the molecules were structured, she recognized rock and dirt and nothing else. The only thing odd was several round spheres layered like mini jaw-breaker candies scattered all in one area. The cold fire of the curse was inside the rocks and several inches down into the soil but no farther.

She stopped her magical observations and felt nauseous for a moment while her vision snapped back to normal. It was only then she realized she wasn't alone. Zavier and Walter were both sitting in wolf form beside her. Zavier scratched in the dirt. "*Did you break it?*"

"*No.*" She had a hunch as to what had been under that pile of rocks but she couldn't verify it in wolf form. She looked around. Other than the three of them, she didn't see another living thing. Zavier didn't know about her odd transformation power, but he knew she had magic. Hopefully he would just assume her ability to transform with her clothes was part of it, which it was.

She transformed. The way his jaw dropped made him look like a cartoon wolf instead of a real one. She pretended she didn't notice and started removing rocks from the pile.

"I can see and smell the curse under this pile of rocks and I think I know why."

She tried not to think about how the pearl she reached for had once been on a dead body that had rotted into the ground around it. Did archeologists ever think about it? At least it looked clean, she thought while she held it up for Walter and Zavier to see.

"I don't think he just used animals. There was a woman here."

Out of curiosity, she focused her new-found sight onto the pearl. There were flames coming off it like it was a little burning coal, but she couldn't feel anything. "I wonder if anyone has ever tried to remove the dirt from inside the curse boundaries. I can see the curse on this pearl. Let's see if anything happens when we take it off the property."

She wasn't sure it was safe to transform with a cursed pearl in her pocket. She didn't want to send the pearl to wherever he clothes went and have it think she owned it. She opted to walk back out even though it was a lot harder to get through the snow in human form than in wolf. She stopped ten feet after they'd crossed the border again. The pearl still burned although the fire had taken on a greenish tinge.

"I don't own you," she told the pearl. "Just taking you on a little field trip. I'll take you back now." She set it just inside the border. She hoped it believed her. She transformed into a wolf again for the trip back to the truck.

When they got back to the truck, she transformed again and got the engine started while the boys got dressed. Zavier pulled himself into the driver's seat and gave an exaggerated shiver before turning to her.

"I am so jealous right now."

She responded with a big, toothy, grin.

"How long have you been able to transform like that?"

"Since I was six."

"Six?! Over-achiever."

"Did the experiment work? Could you still see the curse on the pearl?" Walter asked, sliding into the passenger seat beside her.

"I could. It got a greenish tinge which probably isn't good, but yeah."

"Do you think you're cursed now," Zavier asked in concern.

"I guess if we have a flat tire on the way back, we'll know. I shouldn't be. I put the pearl back."

"Does this mean all we have to do is remove the dirt that's been cursed," Walter asked.

"I don't think it will be that easy. This guy had years to plan the curse. He probably accounted for every scenario. Plus, you'd have to remove the dirt before you bought it or else you'd still own the dirt. Oh, I get it. He's made it all belong together. You can't separate any part of it. Even if you went in before you bought the property and hauled away the cursed dirt, it knows where it belongs."

"I wonder who the woman was," Zavier said.

"Has anyone ever mentioned the guy's wife," Walter asked.

"I bet he used her to make the blood curse and finished off with a crow just for show," Honey said.

"That's really sad," Zavier said.

"Do you think you can break the curse, Honey?" Walter asked.

"I don't know. It's different than the one in Zavier's head. I just manipulated his molecules but this curse is between molecules. I'm not sure what I need to do."

"Zavier's curse was within his molecules?"

She opened her mouth to say yes but realized that might not be true. Something had been making those molecules spin the wrong way. What if straightening the molecules hadn't fixed him at all? What if the curse was still in there? She dove into his head again and tried viewing it the way she had on the property. There was something between the molecules, but she didn't sense the curse. It was a transparent, flowing liquid that flashed multiple colors as it twisted and played inside his brain. Played? Huh. Maybe it was.

"You're in my head again, aren't you?" Zavier said.

"I was. I'm looking in Walter's now."

"What!"

Walter's was the same way. It had the same colors, the same feel, except it felt like Walter instead of Zavier.

"Honey, get out of my head!" Walter sounded panicky.

"I'm out. Could you feel me?"

"No," he said cautiously. "It was more like you felt closer, if that makes sense."

"It does. Sorry to make you uncomfortable. I can't read your thoughts or anything while I'm in there. I just see blobs spinning and fluid flowing. Yours looks a lot like Zavier's, except it feels like you."

"I have blobs in my brain?"

"We all do. Zavier, I don't know how to break the curse. I can do some research when I get back to school. There's a librarian I can ask."

"Whatever you can do, that would be great. I have to get some money together first anyway, maybe find some sponsors. We don't have to do this around Yellowstone either, it's just such a beautiful place and this is where wolves in trouble tend to go."

"You should talk with Lynn. Maybe she'll have some ideas."

"I'll do that."

11

Honey

The rest of the week sped by. She went on a guided tour in wolf form with her Little friends and some people from their pack. The guide, who was a member of the pack who owned the hotel, knew where all the best views were. Honey wished more than once that she had her phone so she could take a picture, but there was no way she could transform and retrieve it from her pocket with fourteen other wolves around. They came across a pack of wild wolves and for a moment she feared there was going to be a fight, but the wild wolves only sniffed at them, then jogged away. Liam wrote in the snow that the wild wolves were used to wolves with a human scent in their lands and tolerated it as long as they brought food occasionally. She wondered how he knew.

Zavier took her and Maya out on the snow mobiles while Maya's son was napping. He said it was so Maya could learn, but by the way he watched Maya and the way she watched him when he wasn't looking, Honey was pretty sure they were attracted to each other. It was sweet. She sent up a prayer that they'd figure it out.

The hot tub room Zavier had designed was amazing. It had floor to ceiling windows that gave an excellent view of the snow-covered mountains behind the motel, teak wood chairs and trim, and a ceramic floor that looked like wood all around a large sunken tub lit from inside the water with blue lights. Lynn loved it. Bernadette looked as grim in the water as out, even when Lynn handed her a drink that had a little tree instead of a mini umbrella.

On the last day Honey went cross-country skiing with the guys and some people from her pack, including Brayton and his friends and his mom and Bernadette. Malcolm's sense of humor was more dour than Luca's but her stomach hurt from laughing at the both of them by the time they neared the motel. Who knew a bully could be so funny?

They weren't far from the motel when they heard screams followed by yelling. One of the yells sounded like Zavier's. Everyone started skiing as fast as they could toward the motel. Honey moved behind some trees and downwind, then used her magic to enhance her speed to get to the hotel well ahead of anyone else.

Three large men in their forties at least were in the front yard. One was holding a baby car seat. Maya was on her knees pleading with them to let her son go. Zavier was standing between the men and their truck. He looked alpha huge, but it didn't seem to be affecting the men much.

"Stand down, pup," the one with the baby said. "You can have the woman, but this is my son."

"No. That is her son and a member of my pack. You threw them out. You lost all rights."

The man looked around and snorted. Ruth and Terri were there with Ruth's teenage children. Honey guessed Terri's children were inside. Walter had gone skiing with Honey and her friends. "This is a pack? This is nothing but women and children. Move or you will die and we will take them with us."

Honey froze the men. She would have frozen everyone so there would be no witnesses but she didn't want to weaken herself too much. She quickly unclipped her shoes from the skis and ran out from behind the corner of the building to jerk the baby from the man's hand and give to Maya. "Terri, take Maya inside and lock the doors."

"What happened to them?" Ruth asked, approaching one of the men slowly while Terri helped Maya up.

"They are temporarily stunned," Honey said. She tapped her chest like she had a necklace on. "We have twenty seconds. How can we get them to stay away?"

"Tie them up and throw them off a mountain," Ruby said.

"They'll just come back," Zavier said. "Legally the baby is Maya's, but this alpha is more powerful than I am. I can't physically stop him from taking the baby. We might have to let the baby go to keep everyone else safe."

"Can the wolf council help?" Honey asked.

"I haven't registered the pack yet, but if I were registered, yes."

"Then we just need to win today."

Zavier looked doubtful but she plowed on. "Help is coming. Zavier, let them think that your power did this. Ruth, go back to where you were so they don't realize how much time has passed. I'll be back."

Honey ran back to the building while Ruth and her kids backed up. A few seconds later, the men started to twitch. It took them a few more seconds to fully loosen up and for them to realize they no longer had the baby. The big one in the middle looked around, then spun in a full circle before turning on Zavier and puffing up like the Pillsbury dough boy.

"Where is she?"

Zavier winced. Honey could tell he was fighting, but the man was powerful. "She's … inside."

The man patted him on the shoulder, hard. "Good pup. You'll make a good alpha someday, if you live."

Honey moved out of her hiding place to stand in front of the doors while the brute marched toward them. "No."

"Get out of my way little girl."

"Make me."

He puffed up, but not as big as he had for Zavier. "I said move."

"And I said no."

He puffed up like King Kong and yelled, "Move!"

She yelled back, "NO!"

He lifted his fist to strike her. She kicked him as hard as she could where it counted and followed up with a punch to the throat as he fell. It wouldn't keep it down for long, but it gave her time to tell her friends what was going on when they skied into view. Ruth and her kids were facing off with one of the men while Zavier was handling the one who claimed Maya's child was his. Her friends spread out to help, but she didn't have time to see who went to help who because her opponent started to transform into wolf form.

"None of that now," Bernadette said, sauntering in with a ski and slamming it over his head.

The ski broke.

"Hmm, guess I need a bigger stick."

"Bernie!"

Bernadette held up her hand and Lynn threw the staff Honey had noticed on the bus like a javelin right into it. Honey wasn't sure how Lynn retrieved the staff so fast, but she was glad she did. Especially when Bernadette landed a blow on the nearly transformed alpha and he collapsed onto the ground face first.

"You guys practice that a lot?" Honey asked.

Bernadette shrugged. "She gets bored."

The other two men were surrounded. The one Ruth had taken on was longer fighting. The second one, the one who claimed to be the father of the baby, had gone wolf, but so had Zavier. Their growls and the way they were biting at each other made Honey want to hide.

"We have to do something."

"No," Bernadette said, grabbing Honey's arm. "Zavier is the alpha. That man threatened members of his pack. It is his right and his duty to defend them and punish interlopers as he sees fit."

"But he might be killed!"

"That's part of being an alpha."

Zavier charged the other wolf again. This time he managed to grab the other wolf's throat and flip him on its back. The wolf fought, then finally stilled. She thought for a moment that Zavier had killed him, but when he released the other wolf and stepped back, the wolf rolled to his feet. Quicker than her eye could register what was happening, Zavier slashed across the back of the wolf's leg

114

with his claw. The wolf whimpered and lay down. Zavier shook himself and started to transform.

Honey knew enough about anatomy that she was pretty sure her cousin had just cut through the other wolf's Achilles tendon. "Why did he do that?"

"It was either that or death," Bernadette said. "Zavier chose to be lenient. The man will heal, but his leg will never be the same."

The door to the motel lobby opened behind them and Maya streaked out holding a blanket. She tossed it over Zavier's shoulders before he was completely transformed and knelt beside him. "Alpha Zavier, are you okay. I'm sorry. I'm so sorry I brought this upon you. I didn't mean…"

Zavier pulled her into his arms. "Are you okay? Is Mika okay?"

"We're okay Alpha."

Zavier kissed her temple then hugged her again. "Good. This man will never hurt you again. I was lenient on him this time because I know he has wives and children that depend on him, but if he ever tries to touch you again, I will not give him a second chance."

"Thank you, Alpha."

"Killing him won't stop us from coming for the boy," the second man called out. "The boy belongs to our pack."

"He is not one of yours. His mother and therefore, him are members of my pack. You no longer have any responsibilities toward him," Zavier responded.

"The girl stole him. Children belong to our pack and their fathers until they are of age to decide for themselves."

115

"You forced yourself on her, planted your child in her belly, and then exiled her. That doesn't sound like stealing to me."

"Is that what she told you," the boy's father asked. He'd transformed, but he was still on his hands and knees. In the fading sunlight, the lights from the motel made his pale skin look ghoulish. Combined with the bite and scratch marks slowly dripping blood, especially around his neck, he looked like a zombie. "I did not force her. Her father gave her to me to be my wife. She wasn't exiled. She ran away. We would never send a pregnant woman off to fend for herself."

"No," Maya snarled. "You would have locked me away until I had the baby, then kicked me out."

"You chose exile. You could have chosen to stay."

"I chose exile for both me and my child. We don't need you."

"Every child needs a father and a mother."

"I am his mother and I have the right to name his father."

"Maya, you know that's not how it works. I'm not dead," the naked man said.

"But you could be." She pushed herself out of Zavier's arms and stood tall. She was nervous, Honey could smell it, but she was determined too. "I Maya Fowler, mother of Mika choose Zavier Brandt to be the father of my child." She spun to face him. "Do you accept?"

"She's not telling you everything," the naked man said. "You must take her into your home as your wife and I'm not dead so it doesn't apply."

"I can make that happen," Zavier said with a growl in his voice, "or you can renounce your rights. I assume you have legitimized that too."

"He can," Maya said. "But you defeated him. You have won the right to be Mika's father, if you choose it."

"I do choose it. I would be honored to raise Mika as my son and I will take you as my wife and Luna if you wish, Maya, but only if that's what you want."

"Luna? You would make me your Luna?"

"Of course."

She lowered her head and appeared to shrink although not like an alpha. "I...I need to think about it."

Zavier reached out to rub her upper arm. "There's no rush Maya. It's a big decision. Take your time."

She looked up at him slowly, then abruptly threw herself forward and wrapped him and his blanket in a tight hug that made him wince. "You are a good man Alpha Zavier." She stood up on her tiptoes and pulled him down to peck him on the cheek. "Stay there. I'll be right back."

"She's very dramatic, that one," Maya's husband or former husband said. Honey still wasn't clear on that point.

"How many wives do you have," Zavier asked.

"Including her? Five. She's the youngest. I only accepted her because her father was desperate. He was a good man. Helped me out of a bind once."

"What was her father desperate for?" Zavier asked.

"To see her safely settled before he died. He knew that as soon as he was gone his wives would chase her out. They never liked her mother either." He pointed at his eyes. "Mark of a witch they said. I looked it up. It's just some weird genetic thing." He shivered. He had to be

117

freezing. Honey was surprised he hadn't stayed in wolf form. "Will you let my friend help me? He can patch me up."

"Will you renounce any claim you have on the boy or Maya?" Zavier said.

"The boy is yours. Maya," he sighed. "I don't think she's meant for marriage, but I made a promise."

"What was it?" Zavier asked.

"That I'd take care of her."

"You were trying to take her baby away."

"It was the only way I could think of to get her to follow me back."

"I promise to take care of her whether she chooses to marry or not. I'm her alpha."

"And I failed or I wouldn't be here. I accept your promise. She is dismissed as my wife."

"Thank you. Ruth, get his friend whatever he needs to patch him up and get them out of here."

Maya emerged from the front door of the motel carrying what Honey thought were two blankets, then she realized one was her baby. She tossed the blanket at her former husband, then turned to Zavier. "Here is my son. Claim him and make him yours."

"Ours," Zavier said, "but he is first and foremost yours."

"No. He is ours. I want you to be his father as much as I am his mother. I meant what I said. You are a good man Zavier Brandt. I want my son to be like you."

Zavier shook his head. "Don't say that. There are things you don't know about me."

"And there are things you don't know about me, but I know what I see and what I feel," she tapped her chest, "in here." She lifted the bundle higher. "Claim him. Name him."

"Name him?"

"Give him your name. I don't want him to have mine."

Zavier took the baby in his arms and, looking down tenderly, said in a hushed voice, "I claim you Michail Mathias Brandt as my son," then kissed the baby's forehead.

12

Honey

They left Wyoming in plenty of time to get back late Saturday but there are a lot of things to see between Indiana and Yellowstone. They also had a flat tire, but Honey didn't think it was due to the curse since it was on the other bus. They pulled into the campus parking lot after dark Sunday night.

Monday was sunny and warm enough to go without a jacket as long as you had a hoodie. Honey was nearly to chemistry class when her phone dinged. Dinged, not trumpeted or banged or exploded. She'd finally come up with a pass code that Luca hadn't been able to crack and she made sure he never saw her use it. It was Alpha Silver, again, better known as BD on her phone. She'd convinced him to use a prepaid phone to contact her, but she wasn't sure how secure that really was since he had texted her every day since he got it. Considering she'd only heard from her dad-dad whenever he dropped by, it was a little weird to have a man who was basically a stranger contact her every day.

BD: Get back okay?

Me: Yep.

BD: When can I see you again?

Me: I'm flying to Texas Thursday night for the Games, so not this weekend.

BD: I'll be there. I'm bringing my wife. She knows. She wants to meet you.

Me: Everything???

BD: No.

Me: Was she mad?

BD: Shocked, but she came round. She's a good woman.

"Who's BD?" Brayton asked.

She jumped so much she nearly dropped her phone. "Don't do that!"

"What, stand on the sidewalk?"

"You snuck up on me."

He smirked. "No, you were about to run into me. Texting while walking – it's dangerous."

She turned her back on him and quickly texted a 'gotta go,' then turned off her phone.

"So who's BD?" Brayton asked again as he stepped forward to open the door for her.

"Don't worry about it."

"Worry? Should I be worried?" He looked concerned but she suspected he was playing with her. It was hard to tell with him.

"I just told you not to be."

"Oh right, you did." They were half-way down the hall before he spoke again. "Who's BD? I can't think of anyone whose initials are BD."

"Stop thinking so hard. You're going to hurt yourself."

He gave her a sly grin that for some reason made her feel like there were butterflies in her stomach. He'd been giving her that grin a lot lately. Could he tell how he affected her? "You could just tell me who it is."

"And you could just stop asking." She charged up the stairs ahead of him. He followed her, taking the steps two at a time and beating her to the top, but just barely, the cheater.

She growled at him while he laughed, then charged ahead of him into the third-floor hallway only to find Deacon leaning against the wall by the classroom like he was waiting for something. Deacon pushed off the wall to stand in front of Honey before she could enter the room. "Honey, there you are. I was waiting for you."

"What do you want?" Brayton asked, stepping in front of her, his demeanor suddenly much more serious.

Deacon glanced briefly at Brayton, then back to Honey. "Just to chat."

"Hurry. Class is about to start," Honey said.

Deacon snorted. "We have five minutes at least. You are always early. Did you have a nice break?"

"Yes." What was he up to?

"Where did you go? I didn't get to go anywhere. Dad had me working."

Honey shrugged. "Road trip."

"Where?"

"Around."

"How was Zavier?"

She raised an eyebrow at him. He wasn't going to catch her that way. Her mom hadn't raised a fool. "You tell me."

"Why would I know?"

"I don't know. Why did you bring him up?"

Deacon puffed up suddenly. She was already breathing through her mouth but the nasty cologne smell got so bad she could taste it. "Touch your toes!"

She pulled the collar of her hoodie over her face. "Ew. Stop. I can't breathe."

He shrank back to normal. Brayton pushed Honey behind him. "What did you do that for?"

Desperate for relief, Honey buried her nose in the back of Brayton's jacket. He must have just washed it. It smelled like detergent but it wasn't strong enough to cover the scent of him.

"Just testing," Deacon said. "Is it true she can't speak telepathically?"

"Where did you hear that?"

"A little wolf told me. Why are you wiggling like that Brayton? You need to use the little boy's room?"

Brayton turned suddenly and pinned Honey's arms against his chest. She'd stuck them up the back of his jacket to make it easier to press the material to her face. Now she couldn't move.

"Honey, why are you trying to tickle me?"

"I wasn't. I was breathing."

"By putting your arms up my jacket?"

"I was trying to bury my nose."

"In the back of my jacket?"

"Your jacket smells good. He smells like…" that's when she realized it wasn't a cologne. "Deceit. Pain. Dust." She peered around Brayton's arm so she could view Deacon's face. "Do you feel all right?"

"Never better." He looked pale to her though.

"How's your brother?"

"Fine."

"He recovered from his illness?"

"He wasn't really ill, just moping."

"Are you sure, because I smell magic, bad magic or the worst cologne ever made."

"I'm not wearing cologne."

"Anyone give you any gifts or food or drink or soap perhaps?"

"No. We better get to class." He spun around to enter the classroom behind a couple of giggling girls, then looked back over his shoulder at Brayton and her. "You guys gonna stand in the hallway doing whatever that is you're doing all day?"

She jerked her hand free of Brayton's hold and out from under his jacket. She immediately missed his warmth, but Deacon was right, they needed to get to class. The teacher always shut the door the second after class was supposed to start. She was already waiting with her watch.

"Honey, wait," Brayton grabbed her arm before she could move more than a step toward the door and pulled her back in front of him. "I smell good?"

"Better than Deacon."

"Do I always smell good?"

She opened her mouth to say mostly, but he did, in fact always smell good. Even when he was sweaty he smelled good. "Unless you've been cursed."

He stepped closer. His scent swirled around her like he wanted her to smell him. Was that possible? Could wolves control their scent? "And have I been cursed?"

She took a deep breath. Deacon's smell was still there, but only faintly. Brayton smelled like fresh air and, well, male, but he was a good smelling male. She raised her head and opened her eyes. "Not that I can tell."

He groaned like he was in pain and pulled her into a hug. "Do you know what you do to me?" he whispered in her ear.

He was warm and puffy with his jacket on. She wrapped her arms around him and laid her head on his shoulder. He was a good height for that. "Drive you crazy?" she guessed, thinking of all the times he'd gotten angry at her.

"Yes," he breathed against her neck, making shivers go down her spine.

"Brayton Mooney, Honey Smith, I'm closing this door in ten seconds. I suggest you get to your seats and stop making out in the hall."

Honey jerked away from Brayton, her face on fire. "We weren't. It was just a hug. I was cold. He's warm," she protested to the teacher.

"Six seconds."

She ran into the room. Everyone's eyes were on her. She slipped into her seat next to Evie and quickly pulled out her notebook.

"Your face is beet red," Evie whispered.

Honey put her finger over her lips.

"Is he a good kisser?" She looked back in Brayton's direction. "He looks like a good kisser."

"We weren't kissing," Honey hissed under her breath.

The door closed. The teacher walked to the front of the class where the projector was already on. "Class, turn to Chapter 21, Electrochemistry. Unlike what Honey and Brayton were doing in the hall, electrochemistry concerns the interchange of chemical and electrical energy, not physical. We'll cover electrochemistry today and Wednesday and have our second exam on Friday. Since you had plenty of time to study over the break, I know you'll all do great."

If Honey's face got any hotter, she was sure it would burst into flame. She didn't dare look back at Brayton during or after class when she went up to remind the teacher that she needed to take the exam early on Thursday. On the off chance he was waiting for her outside the room or the building, she went out the back door of the classroom, pulled her scent molecules in tight as soon as there was no one around to notice, and slipped out the back door of the building. As quickly as possible but not so quick someone would take note, she made her way to the library.

The zap the door in the Janitor's closet gave her almost felt friendly, like it was saying hello. Honey headed directly for the shelf from which the librarian had retrieved the book on curses Honey had read the first time she'd ever come to the library. Some of the books in the surprisingly large section looked well-used. She chose a big, black one that had the air of a reference book. She had pried it half-way out when it felt like something pinched her. Startled, she jerked her hand back. The book fell onto the floor spine first and fell open to a page titled 'The Inside-Out Curse'. The picture was hand-drawn, but she still had to look away. That's when she heard a faint rattle that signaled the rapid approach of the librarian. And it was rapid. The woman was nearly at a full sprint.

"You must leave, quickly." Ms. Carrier looked back over her shoulder, then scooped up the book off the floor and shoved it back on the shelf. "Go."

"But I need a book on curses. Blood curses. There's some land that's been cursed and I told my friend I'd see if I could find a way to break it."

Ms. Carrier scanned the shelf and pulled a thick red one down from the top shelf and shoved it at her. "Take it and go."

"Out of the library?"

"Yes."

"But you said I can't take a book unless I check it out and that if I tried I'd get banished. I don't want to be banished."

"It's officially checked out. You're good. Now get out of here before something bad happens."

"What's going on?"

"Go. Please." The librarian looked over her shoulder, then leaned forward and whispered, "There are people in the library searching the maps for my friend's daughter. They know her name. Go." She gave Honey a meaningful look.

"It's Honey," she mouthed when Honey didn't move.

Honey nodded and ran for the door. How did the librarian know who she was? Had she always known?

Searching the maps probably meant they were doing a location spell with a seeking crystal. From what she remembered of her mom's lessons, how close it got was limited by the map. You usually started with a very general one, like a globe or a country, then worked your way down. You had to use paper maps because magical crystals scrambled the pictures on computer screens permanently. There were spells you could use to keep people from finding you, but her mom had never taught her those. She should have asked for a book on blocking spells while she was in the library instead of one on curses. Ugh. Maybe her witch friends could help.

She ran all the way back to the dorm imaging a large, pointy crystal chasing her across a map of the campus. Blaze wasn't in their room, nor could she find anyone in the hallway. She sent out a message as a group text to all her volleyball friends asking if anyone knew how to block a location spell. Her phone started dinging a few seconds later.

Gorgeous Gloria: *I have a plant for that. Come to my room.*

Lucalicious: *Who's trying to find you?*

Nate-the-great: *That's illegal.*

Weird Walter: *You need help?*

Lively Impassive Amazonian Man: *What did you do?*

Luca had figured out her password again. Darn.

She raced to Gloria's room. Gloria handed her a purple radish.

"What do I do with this?"

"Eat it, leaves and all. It will work for twenty-four hours, then you'll need to eat a fresh one."

"Really?"

She shook a little bag at Honey. "Yep. I have enough seeds for a hundred radishes, so I can protect you for a hundred days."

"Lucky you had this."

"Well, they make a pretty salad too."

"Thank you. Tell me where to get them and I'll buy you some more seeds."

"Cash will be fine. I need to order some other stuff anyway."

Radishes were not one of Honey's favorite food. She could handle them in slices but a whole one, and the leaves – ick. She would have asked if she could add it to a salad with dressing, but time was of the essence, so she choked it down.

"Who's trying to find you?" Gloria asked after Honey had washed down the last bit of leaf.

"I don't know. I went to the special library and the librarian told me what was happening and told me to go."

"That's weird."

"Yeah. Maybe I'll go back after supper and see if she'll tell me more."

"I can go."

"Um, that would be great." The librarian wouldn't tell Gloria her secret, would she? "She was very hush-hush, so I think she was concerned about someone hearing her. Just tell her your friend who checked out a red book earlier wants to know if she can come back."

"Sure."

13

Honey

At seven in the morning, the time Gloria told Honey the librarian had said to come 'have a discussion', Honey was standing outside the main doors to the library. Five minutes after seven, the librarian appeared muttering under her breath about incompetent wolves.

"Come on."

Without waiting to see if Honey was following, Ms. Carrier turned her back on Honey and walked through the main floor of the library to a plain white door with a sign above it that said 'Offices'. Honey followed her down to the very end of the long hallway to the last door before the emergency exit. The engraved nameplate by the door said Mrs. Withers. Under that, a piece of paper was taped to the wall with the name Ms. Carrier written in fancy calligraphy.

The librarian waved her hand in front of the door before opening it and pointing to a worn seat in front of an ancient wooden desk. "Have a seat. I'll pour us some tea. What do you like?"

"Do you have chamomile?"

The librarian frowned at Honey over her shoulder. "'Really? This time of the morning?"

"Whatever you have is fine."

The librarian busied herself in the corner of her office behind and to the side of her desk at a small table with an electric kettle and multiple canisters. After several minutes, she plopped down a reddish-brown drink in front of Honey and nodded at the cup.

"Raspberry."

"Thank you."

Honey's hands were cold from standing outside so she wrapped them around the cup and took a deep sniff. It wasn't just raspberry. Sighing to herself, she put the cup back down without tasting it. "Thanks for seeing me this morning. Can you tell me more about what was going on yesterday?"

"Do you not like raspberry?"

"I like raspberry just fine, just not truth serums with a compulsion spell. I hope you haven't used this on any other wolves."

"No, although I've been tempted," the librarian admitted, looking wryly at the cup.

"The compulsion was a nice touch, you might have gotten more, but wolves are conditioned to talk around the truth if they don't want you to know. We can smell lies so we can't lie to each other."

"You could lie to me though."

"I won't. I believe in the Commandments. If I don't want to answer you, I won't. Besides, don't you have something spelled to detect lies?"

She opened the top drawer to her desk, which Honey hadn't noticed was cracked open, and pulled out a stone.

131

She put it on the desk between them. "Yes, but it doesn't always work."

"My name is George," Honey said.

The rock turned black.

"Looks like it's working to me."

The librarian put her hands together on the desk in front of her and faced Honey head on. "Honey, how old are you?"

"Why do you want to know?"

"Because fourteen years ago, right after I got this job, my best friend, my only friend, came to me and begged me to hide something for her. Despite my better judgment, I did. She disappeared. I didn't hear anything from or about her until a couple of months ago when I found out she was dead. You were there. You saw what was revealed. Those people came back. They had a name – one you're familiar with. It could just be coincidence, but being what you are and where you can go, I suspect it isn't."

"And if it isn't?

"You are cursed."

"Am I?"

"I don't know. Who is your father?"

"I'm not going to tell you that."

"How did your mom die?"

"I don't know exactly. When I found her, both her and my father were on fire."

The librarian covered her mouth. Honey dipped her head. She'd thought if she blurted it out, it would eventually become easier. It hadn't.

"You saw it?"

"Yes."

"Did you start the fire?"

132

"NO! I wasn't there. I was at school."

"You said you were homeschooled."

"I was. My mom thought it was time I started integrating into society. I went to high school for one day."

"How did you end up here?"

"When I found them, I ran like they'd told me to. I was caught by one of the packs and when the Luna heard my SAT score, she gave me a full-ride scholarship to college."

"What was your score?"

Honey looked up at her through her wet lashes to see Ms. Carrier's reaction. "Perfect."

It wasn't much of a reaction. The librarian blinked.

"Is that your power?"

"What?"

"Taking tests."

"That's a power?"

The librarian gave a little shrug. "It's not so much taking tests as it is interpreting what the creator of the test was thinking when he made it."

"Um, no."

"What is it then?"

"A wolf's power is to transform."

"Honey, you look just like her, except for the eyes. I know who your mom was and I know what she was. You aren't just a wolf."

"Are you going to turn me in?"

"I haven't decided."

The rock, which had turned gray again about three seconds after Honey's lie, remained that way. The librarian was being honest at least. Should she tell the librarian she was right? The librarian was her mom's friend, but that was years ago. There was nothing to keep her from turning Honey in. She hadn't yet though. She had even warned Honey yesterday.

"Why didn't you turn me in yesterday?"

"I wasn't a hundred percent sure who you were."

She was probably just protecting herself. If she turned Honey in, the other witches would wonder why the librarian had allowed a wolf into the library. On the other hand, it would be nice if she could be friends with someone her mom had once known. She had to be sure though. Had her mom told Ms. Carrier she had a hybrid child?

"Other than she went into hiding, what makes you think your friend had a child with a wolf? Isn't that forbidden?"

"When she was a sophomore, her grandmother arranged for her to marry the son of a powerful family. He was a good catch on paper and he wasn't bad looking, but I could tell she didn't really like him. She never stated her true feelings of course, at least not where any other witches could hear. I don't think she felt comfortable talking to other witches out of fear it would get back to her grandmother. I think that's why she became such good friends with a wolf. It was dangerous for them to admit knowing each other, so they both knew that whatever was said would be kept confidential."

"Did you like the wolf?"

She shrugged. "He was okay."

"Did he have any friends that knew about the relationship?"

She gave Honey a squint-eyed look. "A brother."

134

"Did you know him?"

She snorted. "How could I not know him? He followed his brother everywhere."

"Did you like him?"

The librarian smiled softly. It made her look a lot younger. "He was funny and mischievous and sweet. My friend and his older brother would dump us and the younger brother would wind up with me. He never seemed to mind. He'd crack jokes until I laughed. If he'd been a witch...," she sighed.

"Did you remain friends with the younger brother after you graduated?"

"I did an accelerated masters in library science. I didn't have time to socialize, then I started working here."

Ms. Carrier had been friends with her dad too but both of them had left her behind. She was lonely. Honey could sense it and smell it. She felt bad keeping everything from her.

"My father was a man name Matt. He wasn't my biological father, but I didn't know that until recently. He found my mom about a month before I was born and basically adopted me as his own. He died with mom."

"He was a wolf?" she asked.

Honey nodded, she couldn't talk through the tears. The librarian tugged a couple of tissues from a box and offered them to her, then grabbed more for herself.

"Okay," the librarian said several minutes later once they'd both gained some control. She took a deep breath and put both hands down on her desk. "Have you ever killed anyone?"

"No."

"Have you ever intentionally hurt someone?"

135

"Not badly."

Ms. Carrier have her a suspicious look.

"It's a wolf thing. I do MMA," I explained.

"What's that?"

"Mixed Martial Arts. Dad, Matt, signed me up for classes starting when I was three. I won the intercollegiate and state competitions. I'm flying to Nationals on Thursday."

"You're good at school and sports?"

"Some of them."

"Hmm. Have you ever hurt anyone on purpose other than for sporting reasons?"

She wracked her brain trying to think of something. She almost said no then she remembered the waitress. "I did whack a waitress against a table a few times, but she was trying to spell Brayton's grandfather to make him force a bunch of wolves to do her will, so I'm going to claim self-defense, but otherwise, I can't think of anything."

"You whacked a waitress?"

"She was a witch. She cursed a couple of wolves. One of them almost killed a bunch of people."

"Okay, we'll call that justified. Anything else?"

"No, I don't think so."

"Any violent urges?"

"Nothing abnormal, if that's what you're asking."

She lowered her eyebrows at Honey again. "What do you mean?"

"I punch my friends when they are acting like idiots. Not hard though."

"Wolf or witch?"

"Wolf mostly. They can take it."

She was quiet for several moments, then let out a sigh. "You should not exist. Your mom, well I suspected, but she never …confirmed."

"Did she say who the child's father was?"

"No, but the timing was right and why else would she have disappeared? Besides, look at you! You're proof."

"If my mom was your friend," Honey pointed out. She hadn't confirmed anything.

Ms. Carrier pulled another stone from her drawer and set it on the desk in front of her. This one was brown and roundish. She tapped the top and Honey smelled iron – an entrapment spell.

"I didn't want to have to do this, but you've left me no choice."

Honey couldn't move. She couldn't even open her mouth. She might have been scared if she wasn't so angry. Ms. Carrier had no right to trap her. She hadn't done anything wrong.

She'd never tried to break any of those spells her friends had thrown at her because she didn't want them to feel her magic, but now... Just in case it would work on a witch, Honey made sure the air shield she'd pulled up while she was walking to the library was still tight around her before focusing on the spell coming from the stone. Unlike at Yellowstone, she didn't need to look between the molecules. The spell was obvious – the molecules were all frozen in space. It was like what she did, but instead of freezing her, the spell had frozen everything around her. That was easy to fix. She willed the molecules around her to start moving again, but remained still to see what the librarian would do. Ms. Carrier had retrieved something small from the shelf behind her and was now holding it up for Honey to see. It looked like a really sharp guitar pick.

"I'm just going to take a little blood."

Honey froze her and left.

14

Honey

The guys were waiting outside when she got back to the dorm. After the group text on Monday, they'd insisted she tell them what was going on. She couldn't tell them anything about the library, of course, but she had told them that a witch friend who was more in touch with what was going on in the witch world had warned her that people were looking for her and that she was going to speak to someone in the library who might be able to help. They'd all been very suspicious. It took her over an hour to convince them not to follow her to the library on Tuesday morning.

Luca was the first one to spot her. He ran ahead and attacked her with a hug. "I'm so glad you're safe." He sniffed, then pushed her back to hold her at arm's length. "Why were you crying and why do you smell angry?"

"Because I *am* angry. She was totally unhelpful."

"Did she try anything?" Walter asked.

"Nothing I couldn't handle."

Liam looked around then said very quietly, "Did you have to use, you know?"

"She froze me and attempted to take my blood. I returned the favor, well, not the blood part."

"Honey!" His admonishment was laced with concern.

"Don't worry. She used a spelled stone to freeze me. I turned it to face her when I left so she would think I just managed to evade the spell."

"That's just as bad."

"No. She already knows magic doesn't work on me."

"What?" All four of them were looking at her in shock.

I shook my head at them. "Her magic, as expected. She never used it on me directly before but she knew I was odd."

"Honey, who is this person," Liam demanded.

"I can't tell you." Well, maybe she could. If she could break the freeze spell, maybe she could also break the one that kept her silent about the library. She'd made a promise though. She didn't want to accidentally tell someone about the library. "I can tell you that she was one of my mom's friends and helped to hide me when I was a baby."

"Hide you?" Nathan asked.

"Yeah. I'm not sure exactly how it works, but when a new witch is born it shows up as a leaf on a big tree. The person I went to speak to hid my leaf. It only recently appeared but it didn't show my name. I don't know how they figured out what my name was, but they have it now, and my age. The person I went to see didn't know for sure that I was who they were looking for. She only knows my name but not my age. She wanted to confirm who I was."

"Why didn't you tell her?" Liam asked.

"Because I didn't trust her not to turn me in."

"Who are the people looking for you?" Walter asked.

"My mother's family, the woman's bosses, I think."

"Would it be that bad if they found you?" Luca asked gently. To him, family was everything and none of his family would ever turn on the rest.

"My mother cut all contact with them and hid for fifteen years to keep them from knowing about me. I think she would know more than anyone how dangerous it was for them to know about me."

"You're right," he sighed. "I wish things weren't like that."

"Me too."

"What are you going to do?" Walter asked.

He asked her like she already had a plan. He knew her well. "If she turns me in, I don't know. Run, I suppose. Otherwise, I'm going to keep eating those radishes until I go to Texas. I'll pause eating them while I'm there, then eat one right before I leave. Hopefully, that will pull them off the scent for a while."

"Do you think she'll turn you in," Walter asked.

"I don't know. She's afraid of the curse, but she was really good friends with my mom. She knew both of my..." she nearly said dads. They guys didn't know she knew who her dad was nor that she had a bio-dad. She wanted to tell them but the risk was too great if someone ever forced them to talk. "...parents."

"She knows who your dad really was?" Luca asked excitedly. "Did she tell you who it is?"

"We never discussed that."

"How did you meet this woman?" Liam asked.

"She works in the library. She has a framed picture of my mom when she graduated and she told me they were friends even though she didn't know who I was."

"You need a plan in case you have to run and a way to hide yourself other than radishes," Walter said.

"I know. I'm working on it as we speak."

And she was. She'd already decided not to go to Yellowstone or Texas, assuming she got to go this weekend. Florida perhaps, or even across the ocean? How did someone get a passport? Maybe she could go to South America. She didn't know where she'd get the radishes though. Gloria could grow them in a day. It would take her months. There had to be a spell or something she could use. Unfortunately, she could no longer use the magical library so there was no way to look it up.

"I'm going to grab some breakfast."

"We'll come too," Walter volunteered.

"You can't protect me. It's not safe."

"They can't do anything to you if they can't find you. We'll help you keep watch. We can take turns going with you to classes and wait outside the door."

"No. You guys have your own stuff to do."

"Not all our classes are at the same time as yours," Luca said. "Besides, I'll be more likely to study if I have to sit in a hall with nothing else to do. We can text you if we see or feel any strange witches coming."

"All witches are strange so that could be a problem," Nathan snarked.

"You guys are the best."

"Group hug!" Luca declared. Normally he was the first one to reach her, but this time it was Walter who got his arms around her first.

She spent the rest of the day waiting for someone to arrest her. She was almost distracted enough not to feel awkward when Brayton walked into Chemistry Lab. She'd managed not to talk to him yesterday at supper by surrounding herself with friends and eating as fast as possible. She was alone here though. Evie hadn't made it to class yet. Honey ducked her head and started digging around in her backpack so she wouldn't have to look at Brayton when he passed. Several seconds later, enough that he had plenty of time to find his seat, she put her bag down.

"Honey?"

She jumped, making the leg of her chair squeak against the floor. Brayton was standing right beside her. She should have realized he was there. His scent was way too strong for him to be in the back of the room.

"Yes, Brayton?"

He touched her shoulder and a pleasant zing went through her. "Honey, look at me."

It was just Brayton. So what if people thought they'd been kissing. Other college students did it all the time. Why was she even worried about what other people thought? She pulled up a smile and flicked it at him. "Yes?"

"Are you mad at me?" He actually looked a little worried.

"No. Why would I be mad?"

"I don't know, but it feels like you've been avoiding me."

"I'm not."

He raised an eyebrow at her.

143

"Well, I'm not now. It wasn't you." She ducked her head to hide her rapidly warming cheeks.

He leaned close enough to block the light and said in a quiet voice, "Don't let the teacher get to you. She's tired and bitter and we provided a convenient target for her anger."

Honey nodded while keeping her face averted.

"So, you want to study for the test later? I could use your help."

"Sure. Lib…Student Union? I'll see if Evie wants to come too and text you with a time."

"Hey." Deacon threw an arm around Brayton's shoulder. "Can I get in on that since we're all *friends* and all."

She hadn't even noticed Deacon come in. She could smell him, just like she smelled other wolves, but the nasty smell was mostly gone.

Brayton lifted Deacon's arm off his shoulder with two fingers and dropped it like it was covered in something nasty. "Don't ever do that again."

"Oh, sorry. Would you rather I kissed you?" He puckered up his lips.

Brayton looked like he was about to punch him.

"You look like one of those fish they find on the bottom of the ocean," Honey said to lighten the mood. "You know, those really ugly ones with teeth and random things sticking off of them everywhere."

Brayton snorted.

Deacon rolled his eyes. "Oh, ha ha. Seriously though, mind if I study with you?"

Brayton looked at her. She shrugged.

"I'll text you when she texts me," Brayton said.

Brayton and Deacon moved toward their bench. Evie stumbled into the classroom. Her nose was red and her eyes half-closed. She wiped her nose with a crumpled tissue and plopped down next to Honey.

"You don't look good," Honey said.

"I don't feel good."

Honey reached over and felt her head. "You have a fever. You should go back to your dorm."

"I only have two classes today. The medicine should kick in soon."

Honey wished she had her mom's power to make her friend feel better. Hmm, maybe she did. It wouldn't be magic, but her mom often sold combinations of herbs that helped with colds and flu. Honey had helped her mix them, so she knew what they were made of. "Which dorm are you in? I can mix up an herbal tea that might help."

Either Evie's medicine never kicked in or she was sicker than she realized. She nearly caught their battery on fire by hooking up the wires wrong and stabbed herself with the electrode she was about to poke into the lemon when she sneezed. Honey bandaged her up with the first aid kit, then made her take notes while she finished up.

She didn't bother asking Evie if she wanted to study.

15

Brayton

Honey walked into the student union with Luca, Liam, and Walter with a smile on her face. For a moment Brayton thought they were going to study with them too, but Honey nodded toward them, returned Luca's hug, and started his way alone, without her smile.

"Is she dating that short guy?" Deacon asked.

Brayton shrugged.

Honey pulled out a chair and plopped her backpack on the table. "Evie's not coming. She's still sick."

"Still?" Brayton asked. He'd noticed the human was sneezing a lot during lab yesterday and that Honey was sitting by herself in class earlier, but he hadn't thought much about it.

"Yeah. I think she has the flu." She pulled out her chemistry book and plopped it on the table. "How do you guys want to do this? I've already written an exam. We can all take it then compare answers."

"You've done what now?" Deacon asked.

"Written an exam. I pretend I'm the teacher while I'm going through the notes and write an exam, then test myself on it the next day to see how I do."

She really was a nerd. He hadn't looked at his notes since he'd taken them. "I don't think I'm ready for that."

"I have flash cards too, if you want me to quiz you."

She had flash cards. Of course, she did. "Why don't I quiz you?"

"Okay." She pulled out a deck of bright yellow cards. "Shall we do it Jeopardy-style?"

"Jeopardy-style?"

"Yeah, you read and Deacon and I buzz in by slapping the table. We get a point every time we get a question right. The loser gets to buy the winner a fancy coffee or a cookie from Coffee and Crumbs."

"Maybe you should read the questions and Brayton and I should compete," Deacon said.

Honey tapped the edge of the cards on the table so that the edges were all perfectly aligned. "That sounds fair since I made the cards. You get five seconds to answer. If you can't answer and I can, I get the points."

He was going to lose, although he didn't think Deacon would do much better. "Actually Honey, can we go over the questions from the chapters? I don't understand how they got some of the answers in the book."

"Sure."

Deacon raised an eyebrow at him while Honey dug in her backpack for a notebook. Brayton ignored it. Sure, he might have laughed behind some smart kids' backs a few times, but that was when he was younger and stupid. So what if Honey took her studying seriously.

Her green eyes looked up from her notebook and he caught a whiff of her scent at the same time. His brain stuttered.

"Which chapter do you want to start with?"

Chapter? "Uh."

"Just start with whatever is on the test," Deacon suggested.

Something dinged in Deacon's backpack. He pulled out his phone and touched the screen, then tossed it back in his bag. "Sorry, I've got to go."

"We haven't even gotten started," Honey said.

"I'll have to take a rain check."

"I guess it's just you and me then, Brayton," Honey said. She didn't look happy about it.

"Good, you can focus on helping me. Let's look at the first question."

Honey's phone buzzed. He couldn't see what it said, but after reading the message, she glanced toward the door then starting shoving things in her bag.

"What are you doing?"

"Sorry Brayton, I have to run."

"But we just got here."

"I know. I'm sorry."

"Can we meet later? I really need your help."

She opened her mouth to answer, but Luca sprinted out of nowhere and started pulling and tugging her away. Honey took another look toward the front door and started running with him toward the back stairs. Just as they disappeared, a tall woman in a long, straight skirt and a frilly, silky-looking top stepped through the main door. Even from where he sat, he could smell the magic on her. It smelled just like Honey had that one day she disappeared and claimed she'd been in the library. The woman scanned each table, clearly looking for someone or something.

What had Honey done now?

16

Honey

"It's all clear. Come on."

Luca pushed open the back door of the Union and they walked out calmly like they hadn't just been running from someone. Walter and Liam joined them about halfway back to the dorms.

"Who was that?" Walter asked.

"The librarian who was my mom's friend. Did you see anyone else?"

"I didn't," he said.

"How did she know where you were?" Liam asked.

"I don't know."

"Maybe she was looking for someone else," Luca said.

"It's possible."

"Are there ways witches can find people other than a seeking crystal?" Walter asked.

"Yes, but the seeking crystal is the only one that points to people from long distances, I think."

"We need to know, Honey. Ask your witch friends," Liam said.

"I will."

Speaking of witch friends, she wondered if the librarian knew which dorm Gloria lived in. Shoot, Ms. Carrier knew who Honey's roommate was thanks to her attempt to join a coven. The librarian also knew she was leaving for the weekend to go to Texas. Honey sent up another prayer that the librarian wouldn't turn her in. Would it be safer if she didn't sleep in her dorm tonight?

"Guys, can I sleep on your couch tonight? She might know where I live."

"You think she means you harm?" Liam asked.

"I don't know what she wants. I just know I don't want her to get any blood."

"What about hair?" Luca asked.

"Hair?"

"Yeah, you know like in Star Trek when that doctor turned old. They found some hair in a hairbrush to fix her DNA so she could be young again."

"Fingernails. I heard witches could use fingernails," Walter said.

"What kind of a slob do you think I am? Who leaves their fingernails lying around?"

"What about a piece of clothing? Can they track you with that?" Liam asked.

"A wolf could," Luca stated, "if you'd worn it recently."

"These are witches, but they might be able to use it," Honey concurred.

"We'll escort you to your dorm room. You can grab anything they might be able to locate you with and bring it to our rooms," Walter said.

"Grab your pillow and your sleeping bag," Luca said. "Actually, you should strip the bed. The sheets will smell like you too."

"Okay. Thanks guys. I really appreciate this."

"We know," Luca said.

Blaze wasn't in their room. Honey stuffed all her bedding into a pillowcase, threw all her laundry in the washer down in the basement, and grabbed all the clothes she thought she'd need for the next week. By the time she was done grabbing everything else, it looked like no one lived there but Blaze.

She stayed in the basement to wait for her laundry to dry while the boys carried everything else to their dorm. Since she wasn't carrying anything, in theory, no one should realize she was temporarily moving in. Liam came down to join her after they were done.

"I thought you had a chemistry test tomorrow," he said moving the book on the couch so he could sit near her.

"History comes first."

"Honey, we need to talk."

"What about?" She had a feeling she knew exactly what he was going to say.

"How many people know what you are?"

She was very careful to word her answer so she wouldn't have to tell him about Alpha Silver. If the guys knew her bio-dad was alive and were forced to say something, it could destroy her bio-dad's whole pack.

"I've only told you guys and I'm sorry now that I did. I didn't realize you could get in trouble just for knowing."

"It's all right. If it comes to that, I have prepared an explanation as to why we didn't turn you in."

"You have?"

"Yeah. I've done a lot of research Honey. You don't have any signs of being the monster that other wolches have been before. My guess is it's because your mother was a healer. That's what I'm going to say anyway. We'll say we were keeping an eye on you and that we would have turned you in if we thought you were dangerous. We're just a bunch of teenagers so I don't think we'll be severely punished. I prefer not to get caught and find out I'm wrong though."

"I prefer you not get caught at all."

"Me too, which is why we can't let the witches find you. There's got to be a magical way to hide you."

"But I can't look it up because the librarian will be waiting for me," she sighed.

"Here, but you're going to be in Texas and there's a famous witch college there."

"There is?"

He grinned and handed her a note card. "One of my witch friends told me."

"You mean our?"

"Nope. He's a sophomore in one of my classes. He's my lab mate. No one else would sit by him. He knows that you have witch friends and that I'm your friend but he's never met you and I didn't mention you when I asked about other witch schools."

She leaned over and gave him a one-armed hug. "You're the best Liam."

He hugged her back. "I know."

Her phone dinged. Brayton, again. He'd sounded pretty desperate when he said he needed help and she wouldn't be able to help him tomorrow. She unlocked her phone.

BB: Answer me Honey. What's going on?

Me: I might have pissed off a librarian.

BB: What did you do?

Me: Not important. I can meet you in your suite in an hour if you still want to study.

BB: An hour?

Me: I'm doing laundry.

BB: *OK*

Trying to help Brayton was a mistake. He kept questioning her about the librarian until she told him she would leave if he mentioned it again. Then, he started giving her puppy-dog eyes every time he looked up from a problem. He was nearly as good as Luca at begging. Luckily, she only had to resist for ninety minutes. That's how much time she had allotted to help him. She started collecting her things at exactly nine.

"You're going?" He topped the hurt in his voice off with a pout. "We haven't gone through everything yet."

"I have another test to study for and some homework to finish."

His pout transformed into a slow grin that made her belly butterflies all take off at once. "How about tomorrow?"

"I'm sorry." She truly was. Except for his wheedling, she had enjoyed talking chemistry with him, "I won't have time. I'm flying to Texas with the rest of the track team after classes." He knew that.

"Your classes are all early though. You should have a little time in the afternoon."

"I'll be taking the chemistry exam then and I promised I wouldn't tell any of the other students what was on it."

He released a displeased huff. "Oh. Well, I'll escort you to your dorm then."

"No need. I'm going upstairs."

She sensed rather than saw Cici glare at her from the end of the couch where she'd had her head buried in a book the whole time. What was her problem?

"You can stay down here and study if you want. I make a mean microwave chocolate chip cookie," Brayton said.

"By mean, he means you'll be lucky if you don't break your teeth," Malcolm yelled from his room.

"I think I'll pass." She turned her back on him and slid her backpack onto her shoulder at the same time. Somehow, he beat her to the door.

"After you." He gestured grandly toward the opening.

"Thanks."

He closed the door after her like she expected, but he was on the wrong side. She gave him the benefit of the doubt and didn't say anything at first, but when he started following her up the stairs, she knew he was up to something.

She turned and scowled down at him. "Why are you following me?"

"Someone has to protect you from irate librarians."

"She's not going to look for me in a boys' dorm."

"Better safe than sorry."

"Brayton, I don't need you to protect me."

"If you'd just tell me what's going on I could decide that for myself."

She rolled her eyes. "Brayton, it's just a librarian. She's gone home by now."

He shrugged and pushed past her. "Maybe I just want to go up to the third floor."

She squeezed past him and ran the rest of the way up the stairs and down the hall. If Brayton saw all her things in the boys' room, he'd badger her all night. He didn't chase her, but Nathan took his time answering the door, so Brayton was standing with her by the time Nathan opened it.

"Hey Honey, you're home." He stepped aside to let her in. Brayton followed without waiting for an invite. Nathan didn't try to stop him.

Her worries were unfounded. The boys, bless them, had stashed most of her things in their rooms. Only the pillowcase of bedding leaning against the wall by the couch and a pile of books on the coffee table were apparent.

"You guys decide to finish studying up here?" Nathan asked.

"Yep," Brayton said, plopping down on the couch next to Luca and pulling out a book. She hadn't even noticed he had his chemistry book under his arm. If he thought she was going to sit next to him, he was dead wrong.

"Nope," she informed Nathan. "I came to study history with you." They had different sections, but they were in the same class.

"Good, I just finished my cards." He pulled a handfull of blue note cards out of his pocket.

She pulled the ones she'd made out of her backpack and waved them. "Me too."

"Shall we go to my room so we don't disturb anyone out here?"

"Um," she glanced at Brayton. He had his nose buried innocently in the book, but she could tell from the thickness of the pages that he wasn't in the right section. She knew what he was up to. He was going to quiz Luca with a little alpha power to get his answers. "Let's stay out here. We can talk quietly."

Brayton squinted his eyes at her while she and Nathan sat on the floor on the other side of the coffee table, then turned to Luca. "So, Luca, what did Honey do to make a librarian mad?"

Luca looked cautiously from Brayton to Honey and back. "Was she mad?"

"You tell me."

Luca shrugged, "I couldn't tell."

"Did Honey steal a magical book from her?"

"Not that I know of."

"Why was she chasing her then?"

"I don't know."

"Yet you knew she was coming."

"Not really."

Brayton didn't look convinced, but they could all smell Luca wasn't lying.

"Nathan?" Brayton snapped.

"Same answers."

Luca and Nathan's heads dipped while Brayton started swelling. "I want some answers and I want them now! Who was that woman and why was she chasing Honey?"

Honey slammed her hand on the coffee table to pull his attention to her. "Stop it Brayton! Stop bullying my friends. They don't know."

"Do you know?"

"Not completely."

"Tell me what you know."

"Turn off your power."

"Will you tell me then?"

"Turn off your power."

"You are in my pack. It is my job to protect you. How am I supposed to protect you if you don't tell me what's going on?"

"Brayton, I appreciate you wanting to protect me, but holding people I care about hostage with your power is not the way to get me to cooperate."

He crossed his arms.

She considered freezing him and throwing him out in the hallway, but that wouldn't protect her friends while she was in Texas.

"How do I leave your pack? Do I just declare I'm no longer a part of it?"

Brayton's eyebrows lowered to a dangerous level. "You'd do that after everything my mom has done for you?"

"I don't want to, but I will if you don't drop this."

"I'm trying to help you."

"I don't want your help."

"But you'll accept theirs?" He gestured toward her friends.

"Yes."

He closed his eyes for a few moments, then slammed his book shut. "Maybe you should leave our pack then. I'll tell Dad you're considering it."

"Make sure you tell him that it has nothing to do with him and that it's only because I want to protect my friends from your bullying," she said to his back while he stomped toward the door.

He slammed the door behind him so hard the wall shook.

Her stomach was tied up in knots, and her chest hurt. Part of her wanted to chase after him and apologize, but then she'd be right back where she started. She took a deep breath. "Sorry about that."

"You'd really leave the Mooney pack?" Luca asked.

"It would be for their own good. I wish I'd never told you guys what I was either."

Luca jumped up and pulled her into a hug. He always knew when she needed one. "Don't say that Honey. No matter what happens, I'm glad you told me. I'm glad you trusted me enough to share."

Nathan patted her on the shoulder. "Me too, Honey. In fact, you've inspired me. I'm going to write my senior thesis on ways to improve wolf-witch relations. Now come on, let's finish studying so you can get to bed."

17

Honey

She didn't see Brayton or the librarian at all on Thursday, which was fine with her. She took the test, packed her bags, making sure to include the book on curses she'd checked out from the library and the two radishes Gloria had passed her in the cafeteria, then caught the bus to the airport with Liam and the rest of the track team. The wolves who qualified for MMA and OA, including Brayton, would fly out late on Friday.

Just before they took off, she checked her email one last time. There was a message from a strange address literally named 'temporary_email_account'. She knew who it was from as soon as she read it even though there was no signature. "*Scrying worked. They know what you look like. Stay away from witches.*"

How was she supposed to do that? Witches were everywhere and she wouldn't even know they were witches unless they'd recently done magic.

"What's wrong Honey?" Liam asked. He'd sweetly taken the middle seat so she could sit by the window even though it was the first time either of them had been on a plane. She showed him her phone.

"Who's it from?"

"The librarian."

"What does she mean," he pointed to the word scrying and tapped his ear. He didn't have to remind her they were basically sitting in a tin can full of people with abnormally good hearing.

"It's a way to see someone now or later."

"Can they take a screen shot?"

"Or just use their phone."

"And then post it on Snapchat," he finished.

"Something like that." She typed in her notes app and tilted it for him to see. "*Witchat?*"

"Funny."

"What am I going to do?" she said, then typed, "*I can't go into the library in Texas now. They might be looking for me.*"

"You think?"

She nodded. She almost mentioned her family's status, then remembered that he didn't know she knew who her mom was. "She knew I was going somewhere this weekend."

"Surely they don't watch TV all the time."

If anyone was listening to their conversation, they had to be really confused by now.

"No, the show is probably only on once or twice a day."

"It will be fine." He took her phone and typed, "*We'll find you a disguise. Even if they scry while you are wearing it, they won't be able to Witchat fast enough to find you.*"

She elbowed him in appreciation of his attempt to lighten things up.

161

He nodded out the window. "We're starting to move."

"Maybe I could get an ombre wig in purple," she mused as the plane backed past all the service vehicles clustered around the terminal.

"I don't know what that means," Liam said, peering over her head.

"And big glasses with thick frames."

"Like an old lady?"

"A fashionable old lady."

"Whatever you say Honey."

She didn't dare open the book on curses in the plane. After years of exposure to the magic in the library, it reeked. She'd sealed it in a large plastic bag and stuffed it in the bottom of the duffel bag one of the guys had loaned her. Instead, she worked on the history paper that was due in two weeks and admired the clouds.

The 1600 was one of the first races in the morning on Friday. She finished third, but she wasn't far behind the first two girls. Captain Young was confident that with a little more training she'd be able to beat everyone. The long jump wasn't until ten. The whole team was supposed to stick around, but she snuck off to the beauty supply store that was only a few blocks away from the competition. The store didn't have ombre purple, but they did have a shoulder-length light blue wig and a pair of blue-light glasses with dark frames that covered nearly half her face. She also bought a pair of blue contact lenses to hide her green eyes. Back at the meet, she used her phone to look up how to put them in while Liam was competing. He came in fifth.

After he'd changed into something less sand-covered, she and Liam snuck away again and caught a bus that let them off a couple of blocks from the address on the card. Their destination turned out to be an aging Victorian mansion complete with a stone and iron fence not far from the River Walk. A big sign in front announced it was the Opal Lambert House Museum. A smaller sign hanging under the big one proclaimed that tours were canceled indefinitely. She would have thought they had the wrong address except the place reeked of magic.

Honey didn't see anyone around, but she didn't look too closely. She didn't want to attract attention since she was still dressed as herself. She and Liam found a place to eat along the River Walk, which was very nice, then she changed in the bathroom. Her costume included a blue dress and shoes that Luna had insisted on buying even though they were way more girly than Honey typically wore. The darker blue tone turned out to go very well with her light blue wig. The color of her contacts, after she finally managed to get them in, was right in the middle. She thought she looked pretty good considering she got dressed in a bathroom stall. She imagined she was a confident young witch with an irritating ex-boyfriend who was trying to scry her (that was the cover story she and Liam had come up with), pulled her air shield tight to hide her wolf smell (and hopefully the aura that witches could sense), and stepped out of the bathroom.

Heads turned.

Okay, they didn't, to her surprise. Maybe a girl with blue hair wasn't that uncommon. She tried to act like it was perfectly normal way for her to look, but she didn't dare glance at Liam, he'd probably laugh.

She'd forgotten about her backpack. It was black and didn't match her outfit at all, but she couldn't think of a non-suspicious way to leave it for Liam, so she took it with her.

The school was right where they'd left it. She checked to see if anyone was watching, made sure her air shield was as tight as she could make it, then pushed open the low gate and stepped into the yard. She smelled the ward just before she walked through it. It smelled like metal for shielding, cotton for hiding, mothballs for forgetting, skunk for repelling, and a cotton candy scent just for fun?

Beyond the ward, the house looked much the same, but now there were people in the yard sitting on benches under the large shade tree to the side of the house, and on seats on the long wrap-around porch. A woman with white hair and a long skirt that might have been fashionable a hundred- and fifty-years past was already walking toward her.

"Welcome to the Opal Lambert School for Witches and Wizards. How can I help you today?"

"Wizards?"

Nobody called male witches wizards anymore.

"Oh yes, we take everyone. Are you interested in becoming a student?"

"Possibly, but I was hoping to use your library."

The woman cocked her head. "I don't believe you've ever visited us before."

"I haven't."

Honey considered mentioning that a friend of a friend had recommended them, but she didn't want to then have to think up names for those friends if the woman asked.

"What coven are you with?"

The cotton candy smell was getting stronger. Honey had never liked cotton candy. It looked pretty but it was all sticky and icky sweet.

"I'm currently between covens. I don't want to check anything out. I just want to look something up."

"Are you from around here?"

"No. I'm just in town for a few days."

She stepped closer and the smell got stronger. "Visiting someone?"

"No."

The woman floated even closer and Honey had to consciously avoid taking a step back. "Planning revenge on someone?"

"No!"

"What information are you seeking?"

"How to protect myself from scrying eyes."

The woman's eyes sharpened. There was something not quite natural about them. "Someone is scrying you?"

"I think so. I was warned."

"Who warned you?"

"It was an anonymous email." She'd totally blown her storyline, but she had a feeling the woman would have seen through it anyway.

"Did you commit a crime?"

"No."

"Are you running from the law?"

"No." Not yet.

"What type of magic do you possess?"

"Molecular."

The woman abruptly floated backwards and out of Honey's comfort zone. Literally. Her feet didn't touch the ground until she was several feet away. "Follow me please."

The girls sitting in chairs on the porch next to the front door giggled when Honey passed, but it didn't feel mean. One of them, a girl with a head-full of frizzy, orange-colored curls, followed her and the woman inside and into the second room to the right. The room was large but cozy with conveniently placed stuffed armchairs and small study tables. Books covered the walls all the way up to the high ceilings. Rolling ladders made them accessible. The woman glided across the room and pointed to a wide green book on a shelf just above Honey's height. "You'll find the answer in here, chapters 5 through 7."

"Does the book also contain information on protection from seeking?" Honey asked.

"Chapter three."

"Thank you."

"You are quite welcome," the woman said very sweetly as if she'd never interrogated anyone in her life, much less Honey, "If you would like a tour of our lovely school, please let me know."

"I will."

She nodded, then turned and disappeared into a bookcase.

"The look on your face," the girl who followed them in laughed. "I love it when we get visitors."

Honey pulled the book off the shelf. It was heavier than she expected. "That was a very cool spell."

"You could tell? Most people think she's a ghost."

"It was a guess," Honey admitted, although she didn't think ghosts would smell like cotton candy unless they died from over-consumption of it.

166

"So, where are you from?" the girl asked, then blew a huge pink bubble with her gum.

"Up north."

"You're a Yankee?!" She said with an exaggerated Southern accent and clasped her chest.

"People still use that word?"

"Eh," the girl shrugged. "Who's trying to scry you?"

"I'm not sure. I have my guesses, but I'd rather not go into it." Honey sat down at one of the square wooden tables and opened the book, hoping the girl would get the hint.

Instead, the girl sat down beside her and leaned in conspiratorially, "Is it an ex-boyfriend?"

"Why would you think that?"

She tapped the side of her head. "It's a gift. I can always tell when a boy is involved."

Honey decided not to correct her. For all she knew, there was a boy involved, or a man anyway. "Your magic?"

"No. I'm an elemental. Water is my focus."

"Oh. Nice."

"What's yours?"

"It's hard to explain. Want me to show you?" Honey was tempted to freeze her, but it wouldn't last long enough.

"Sure."

"I'll need a cup of water."

"I'll be right back."

Honey quickly flipped to chapter 3 and started reading. Sadly, she only managed a page before the girl was back with a glass filled to the brim with water. Honey froze it while she was still carrying it across the room, then went back to her reading.

167

"Here you go."

"Look at it."

"What? It's just…" the girl's mouth dropped open. "You froze it. You're an elemental too? Why didn't you just say so?"

"Not elemental. Molecular."

"What? There's no such thing."

Honey didn't want to argue. She just wanted to read the book and leave. Liam was going to start worrying about her if she didn't hurry. "I guess I don't know what I am then."

She turned the page. A spell, finally. A shield spell if she was reading it right. Every magical creature had intuitive magic, but spells allowed the magic to be patterned and crafted into something complex, like turning a ball of yarn into a beaded scarf. The beads, aka ingredients, helped hold the spell together.

Not all spells worked for all people. She'd tried some of her mom's healing spells when she was little, but since she wasn't a healer, they never worked. This spell, though, she could easily envision forming the different layers it described.

The girl leaned forward to see what she was looking at and blocked the light at the same time. "You won't be able to do that one."

"Why not?"

"You're a water elemental."

"Won't hurt to try." Honey pulled out her notebook to jot it down.

The girl picked up a blue stone from the base of the lamp on the table and handed it to Honey. "Use this. It's faster."

"What is it?"

The girl gave her an odd look. "A copy stone. Haven't you ever used one?"

"No."

"Let me show you."

The girl pulled the book toward her and ran the stone down the page, then took Honey's notebook and ran the stone down the middle of an empty page. The words appeared in her notebook just like they looked in the book.

"That's neat."

"I'm surprised they don't have these up north."

"They probably do. I just never came across one."

"Not even at school?"

"Nope."

"Huh."

The girl watched Honey intently while she read the next page. It was distracting. "Is there some reason you are watching me so closely?" Honey finally asked. Could the girl feel her wolfiness?

"Oh, sorry. I was just thinking."

"Ah." Honey focused back on her reading.

"Since you're a water elemental, we might be related," the girl continued.

"It's possible."

"What's your last name?"

Smith might be a common name, but she didn't want to take any chances. "I'm sure it's not yours."

"Yeah, there aren't many of us Lamberts."

"Are you related to the Opal the school is named after?"

The girl smiled proudly. "She's my great-great-something-grandmother." She waved her hand around. "This will all be mine someday."

"Was Opal the model for the spell?" Honey asked.

"No, that was one of her daughters, Philomena. I can't remember how many greats she is so I just call her Aunt."

"Was she a water elemental too?"

The girl scrunched her nose. "No. She was a spell-caster."

"It must be nice to come from such a long line of powerful and famous witches."

"It has its advantages," the girl agreed.

Honey had buttered her up, now maybe the girl wouldn't mind if she was rude. "I appreciate you taking time to speak to me, but I have a friend waiting, so I can't stay long. Can you give me a little time to flip through this?"

"Oh, sure, take all the time you need. I'm sorry. I do get chatty sometimes."

"That's all right." The girl got up and started browsing the bookshelves. It was distracting, but after a minute or so Honey forgot she was there.

The first spell she read was the most promising. With a few tweaks it could be used to protect from scrying too. There was also a description of how to detect when someone was attempting to spy on you. She copied that page and took notes on a few others. She had one chapter to go when she felt something bite her arm. She slapped her hand over the pain and looked around for the bug. All she saw was Miss Lambert standing a few feet away looking closely at a large guitar pick-shaped device.

Honey froze everything around and on the pick, including the girl's hand.

"What did you do?" Honey demanded.

"I just took a little blood. I want to see if we are related."

Honey scooted back out of her seat and stood. She didn't growl but the urge to do so must have shown on her face because the girl took a step back. "You did it without my permission."

The girl shrugged while taking a second step back. "My aunt said you were hiding something."

"Everybody hides things for lots of reasons. That means they don't want you to know."

Honey reached for the pick. The girl held it away from her. Either she was immune to Honey's magic or she didn't realize her hand was frozen yet.

"Let me see it. How does it work? What does it do?"

The girl turned so that her shoulder blocked Honey from reaching it. "If you hurt me, my aunt will retaliate."

"I'm not going to hurt you. I need to know what you've done. What is that?"

"It's a tester."

"What does it test for?"

"Bloodlines."

"Who is privy to the information after the testing is done?"

The girl looked puzzled. "What do you mean?"

"Who will see the results? Will it be just you and me or is the tester magically connected to something somewhere?"

"Just you and me and my aunt. She sees everything that goes on in the school."

"And records and reports it to someone?" Honey asked, "Like a hidden camera?"

"Oh, yes," the girl nodded happily. "You can't get anything by her."

Great. Honey looked around for something fireproof and spied a red mug on top of a low shelf. She marched over and peered inside. Empty. She took it to the table and put it upside down. "Here, put your test on this."

"Why?" The girl was holding it in front of her now, watching it eagerly. She still hadn't realized that her hand and the blood were frozen.

"So I can see it too. It's my blood."

"You won't try to do something to it?"

"I won't touch it."

Honey had no idea what would happen if they found out she was a Wixx, probably nothing, but if the test showed she was a wolf, she'd probably never make it out the door.

Honey unfroze the girl's hand while she gently set the tester on top of the cup. She felt bad for tricking the girl. She was nosy, but Honey sensed she was lonely too.

"Any moment now, one or two of the lines will turn red. Blood flows toward the strongest family line or lines." Her voice trembled with excitement.

"What would happen if you tested a human or a person who wasn't from one of the founders?"

She looked at Honey like she'd grown another head. "Who would test a human?"

"It could happen," Honey insisted, thinking hard. "What if you found a dead person and were trying to identify what they were?"

"Oh." She squinted down at the device. "That must be this line with H at the end."

"Is there one for wolves too?"

She curled her nose. "We wouldn't have to use it on them. We'd be able to tell."

"Even if they were dead?"

She shrugged.

There was a line that branched off opposite from where the human one was. That was probably for wolves. Honey concentrated on the air right above the device. She'd learned how to start a fire by rubbing molecules together long ago. Her mom had always made her start their monthly bonfires that way, but it wasn't easy.

"What are you doing?" the girl asked, looking between her and the device. Her air shield must not be completely impermeable to her magic.

"You wanted to see how powerful I am. Watch."

She was afraid for several long seconds that there was a spell on the device that would prevent her from lighting it on fire, but it finally started to warp. She sent more oxygen toward it and let the now highly-static molecules above it get close enough to discharge. It caught fire with an impressive zap.

"No!"

Honey froze her.

The aunt popped out of the wall and floated/walked toward Honey menacingly. "What did you do to my niece?"

"She'll be fine. I just paused her for a few seconds."

"It's not allowed to perform magic on another within these walls without their permission."

"Is taking blood allowed?"

Her eyes flicked to her niece. "No."

Honey sent more oxygen toward the tester. The small flame turned even brighter as the tester curled in on itself and started to turn black.

"You will release her," the apparition demanded.

Honey did. The tester was useless now.

The girl gaped at the tester which was now nothing but a black lump. Honey sent more oxygen to encourage the fire to burn everything that was burnable.

"And you will leave and not come back," the apparition continued.

"As you wish."

Honey moved to get her things.

"Leave them," spell-aunt demanded.

Honey ignored her.

The girl grabbed Honey's arm, but quickly let go when Honey glanced at her hand with a not-so-subtle look. "Leave them. She'll curse you if you don't listen."

"Neither of you have any right to my personal belongings. My phone and my ID and everything are in there."

"Leave your notes then," the girl said.

She really didn't want to. She might not be able to remember the spell well since she hadn't copied it by hand. It wouldn't surprise her if the spell-aunt tried to wipe her mind as she left too. She'd just have to hope she could shield herself enough that the hologram or whatever she was couldn't get in.

"Fine."

She ripped the pages out of her notebook and laid them out on the table page-by-page so they could both see they were still there. It also gave her the opportunity to glance at them one more time.

"I'll escort you out," the girl said after Honey had laid down the last one.

"Okay." An idea had come to her while she was laying out the pages. She didn't know if it would work, but she was going to try. She faced the apparition. "Thank you for letting me read your book and for informing me of your rules. Now I will inform you of mine. If anyone attempts to perform any magic on me without my permission, I will freeze them. It won't hurt anyone living, but I'm not sure what will happen to a spell as powerful as you."

The apparition squinted her eyes at Honey in a manner very like Honey's great-grandmother. "You are threatening me?"

"No. I'm stating my rules so you don't hurt herself. I think you are a marvelous creation and I hold no ill-will towards you."

She focused harder and saw beyond the molecules to the spaces. She could see a faint blue glow where the apparition was standing and in lines around the library too. Some of the lines where brighter than others. The aunt must have spent years laying down her spell and adding power to make it last.

"What are you looking at?" the girl asked.

"Your aunt's spell. She put a lot of work into it."

"Who are you?"

"Leave. Now," the aunt said.

"Gladly."

Honey slung her backpack over her shoulder and marched into the hall. Trying to watch the blue lines and keep up her air shield along with what she hoped was an impermeable helmet of molecules over her skull took a lot of energy. Her helmet worked though, or perhaps the aunt didn't try to erase her memories. She made it through the wards but kept her shields up until she was certain no one was following her. Only then did she find a bathroom and change.

Liam was waiting by the door when she stepped out. He took her backpack and snaked his arm around her shoulders to pull her close. "There you are babe. I thought you'd got lost in there."

Why was he calling her babe? Her confusion must have shown because he gave a tiny nod to a table not far from the bathroom door populated by two girls and guy. They looked normal enough, but they were watching them through the corners of their eyes while pretending they weren't noticing them at all. Witches.

She let Liam steer her away from them and toward the front door.

"Did they follow me inside?" She asked as soon as they were clear of the restaurant.

"Not immediately. Their phones all buzzed. They read their screens, then started looking around. I heard one of them ask a waitress if anyone with blue hair had been by."

"Phooey. I liked that wig."

"So, what did you find out? Anything?"

That was Liam. Always to the point. Luca and Nathan would have teased her first and Walter would have told her how she looked and then teased her.

She told him everything, then they googled a grocery store and a natural wellness shop to look for ingredients.

18

Honey

Honey had never tried to cast a spell for real before. Sure, she'd copied her mom when she did her healing spells, but that was when she was a little kid. She'd never felt her magic do anything with those spells. This one was different. She could feel her magic trying to hold the pieces together when she constructed the spell on her chosen object and she could feel it when it failed. One thing would fall out of place and the whole mess would collapse like a tower of Jenga blocks. She'd end up staring, again, at a bunch of herbs scattered around a hair tie on a newspaper.

"Any luck?" Liam asked kindly, for at least the tenth time.

"Stop asking," she snapped, then quickly followed with, "Sorry. I failed. Again."

"Maybe we should call it a day. The sun will be down soon."

She looked up from the asphalt of the top floor of the parking garage to see the sky had turned a brilliant orange and blue.

She shook her head. "I was really close that time. I had one more step to go," assuming she'd remembered them all.

"Maybe you should try to spell something hard instead of a hair tie, like a rock."

"It shouldn't matter. Mom used to spell soft things all the time."

He pulled a quarter out of his pocket and handed it to her. "Just give it a try."

She did. She failed.

Liam squatted down beside her while she was rubbing her face and giving herself a pep talk. It's hard to take yourself seriously when you can smell your own lies.

"Hey, it's okay. You've done a lot today. We can try again tomorrow when you're rested. You'll figure it out."

"I need to do it now. What if they scry me while I'm fighting?"

"Can't witches fight?"

She shrugged. "I guess. I don't know any who do, although I think Sabine would like to learn."

"The chances of them seeing you in a middle of a fight are slim. Just try and sit where they can't tell what you're doing or where you are."

"What if I don't figure this out?"

"Then we'll have to buy more wigs. Maybe a pink pixie-cut next time?"

"Um, no."

"I think you'd look adorable," he cooed while shoving the spell ingredients into a grocery bag.

"Ooo – you could borrow it," she said in retaliation. "With your dark skin and square jaw, it'd be perfect. Charlize wouldn't be able to take her eyes off you."

He snorted. "I'll say."

They walked the block or so back to the Riverwalk. Compared to the pavement-covered ground at street level, the walk was an oasis of plants and lights reflecting off gentle waves. It was the perfect temperature too. San Antonio was much warmer than Indianapolis. After a dinner at an outside table, they followed the river back to the hotel. She meant to take a shower and change before going to bed, but she made the mistake of resting for a moment and fell asleep on top of the covers, still in her running clothes.

At 3:59 am., two hours earlier than she'd planned, Honey abruptly snapped awake. Why? She had no idea. Except for the gentle breathing of her roommate, everything was quiet. She tried to go back to sleep, but after ten unsuccessful minutes, she decided one more attempt with the spell couldn't hurt. It would be a disaster if the witches scried her during a fight and realized she was something other than a witch.

She dragged her backpack off the bed and silently slid open the door to the balcony. After pulling the drapes shut and closing the sliding door, she sat quietly for a minute in case she'd disturbed her roommate. Honey still didn't know her name. All she knew was that her roommate was a Junior from Ohio and that she was supposed to run the 100 and the 200. Honey wondered how she'd done.

The night was quiet and cool with the tiniest of breezes. Attempting a spell on the balcony of a wolf-owned hotel full of wolves with no wind to blow it away wasn't smart. She was outside though, and it was very early. If the smell woke someone up, hopefully they'd think some random passing witch had conjured a spell. Besides, she only had enough for one or maybe two more tries.

What was she doing wrong? She'd tried using the flowing hand movements her mom had used to direct her magic, and it had worked, but there was clearly something she was missing. Her mom never had trouble casting spells, even ones she didn't use very often. She'd told Honey once that her mathematical ability probably helped. You had to picture the pieces of a spell in the right places, then use your magic to lasso the pieces and bind them to the object you were spelling.

Wait. Her mom had never said anything about layering spells. Maybe that's what she was doing wrong. She had to put the spell together first and then apply it to her object.

Honey still had Liam's quarter, but she really wanted to use the hair tie. She might not always have pockets for a quarter, but she should always have something to put a hair tie on. She opted to give the hair tie one more try.

The shield spell worked! She could smell the spell *and* see it if she focused enough. Oh, but that meant other wolves would be able to smell it too. Now she needed a spell to keep wolves from smelling it.

The shield spell protected her from scrying with ground mirror and from seeking with shredded map. She had enough ingredients for one more shield spell and she knew two spells on one object were possible - her mom had done it all the time. If she substituted the mirror and map with something wolves didn't like, it should protect her from wolf noses.

What was something wolves found overpowering that she had on hand? There wasn't a single thing in her bag.

She couldn't think of anything in the room either. The shampoo had only a subtle smell. Maybe there was some cleaner somewhere in the hotel. She always had to open the windows even in the middle of winter when it was her turn to clean the bathroom, to her mom's dismay. A truck passed and she got a strong whiff of diesel. That would work too. She just had to wait for the wind to blow perfectly when another truck came by and put the spell together at just the right time. How long would that be and what if she didn't get the timing right?

Smoke would work, especially plastic smoke and she just happened to have a pen in her bag. She also needed something to protect from witch senses in case they had a spell-detector at the MMA competition. They'd had one at the track competition. That was tough. What could counter a spell detector?

Honey sat there for at least ten minutes trying to think of something before she realized it was the easiest problem to solve. She just needed something that wasn't a spell, and that could be anything.

She did the spell again with her two new ingredients and it seemed to work. She could still see the spell but she couldn't smell it. She slipped the hair tie onto her wrist and did a happy dance there on the balcony. After stuffing what was left of her ingredients back into her bag on top of the blue dress that had been crammed in there since yesterday, she went back inside. It was still fifteen minutes till five. She had a whole hour to sleep. Honey laid down on her bed and closed her eyes.

19

Brayton

Brayton glanced toward the elevators again. No Honey. He checked his phone. She hadn't replied to his texts either.

"Where's your partner?"

Coach Peters looked tired, but from the huge mug of coffee he was sipping, Brayton was sure he would soon be his normal over-energetic self.

"I don't know."

"Better find her. The bus will be here in thirty minutes."

He sent another text. '*Coach says get down here.*'

Nothing.

He hadn't talked to Honey since they'd fought Wednesday evening and every moment since then felt wrong. He didn't like that she was mad at him or that it bothered him so much or that the longer she ignored him, the worse he felt. He marched over to the front desk.

"Can you tell me what room Honey Smith is in? I need to make sure she's up. We have to catch the bus in thirty minutes."

"I'll give her a wake-up call," the woman behind the desk said politely.

That wasn't what he wanted, but it was probably for the best. At this point, he'd either yell at her or get down on his knees and beg for forgiveness. Either one would cause a scene.

"I got her roommate," the woman said, hanging up the phone. "Honey was still asleep. It's a good thing you had me call."

"Thank you."

Why was she still asleep? Honey never slept in late. Even when she didn't have to get up for anything, she was always up abnormally early.

He sat down on a couch where he could watch both the stairs and the elevators. Twenty minutes later, his heart gave an extra thump when a dark head emerged out of the stairwell. Honey still looked groggy, but her hair was braided and she had her bag slung over her shoulder like she was ready to go. She glanced out the front door, then headed for the free breakfast laid out in the other room. His couch was between the stairs and the food but instead of looking his way, she waved at someone behind him, then ran past him with a big grin on her face.

"I did it! I did it!"

Brayton turned around just in time to see Liam swing her around in a hug. He looked just as happy to see her as she was to see him. "That's excellent. See, I told you, you could do it. Did you use the quarter?"

"Nope. The secret was to make it before it was applied rather than apply while making it."

What secret were they talking about? What did Liam know that he didn't?

Liam put an arm around Honey and hugged her again. "That's my girl. Have you had anything to eat yet?"

His girl? Pain shot up his arms. Brayton forced himself to uncurl his hands and retract the claws piercing his palms.

"No. The bus will be here momentarily, so I have to eat fast."

"Grab something and take it with you. I'll bring extra in case it's not enough."

"You're coming?"

The excitement in Honey's voice hurt his heart. She never sounded that excited to hear he was going to be around.

"Of course."

Brayton waited patiently for her to notice him when they lined up to get on the bus. She knew he was there. She had to. He could always sense when she was close or looking at him and he couldn't keep his eyes off her, even though he was trying not to look.

A tall, muscular guy that looked somewhat familiar squeezed into line ahead of him, cutting off his line of sight to Honey. Jerk. It wasn't like they were going to run out of seats. Honey boarded ahead of them both and slid into a window seat near the front middle of the bus. It amused him despite the angst she was causing him. She'd sat in the front, just like she did in the classroom. At least that made it unlikely anyone would sit next to her before he got there.

He was wrong. Cut-in-line jerk-face dropped down beside her with an eager grin just before he got there.

"Hi Honey."

And he knew her. Of course, he did.

184

"Hello?" He couldn't see Honey's face behind the tall bus seat, but he could hear the puzzlement in her voice.

Ha. She didn't know him. Brayton could tell the jerk to take a hike.

"You don't remember me do you?" jerk-face smarmed.

"You look familiar, but I can't remember why."

"How's your arm?"

Brayton was now close enough to see Honey's face brighten, darn-it.

"I remember now. You were going to fight Brayton but he got knocked out. You're from Michigan."

"That's right."

"Excuse me, I need to talk to Honey," Brayton said a lot more politely than he wanted to.

"I'm sure there will be plenty of time once we get to the arena," jerk-face said.

"She's in my pack. I'm her future alpha. I need to speak to her."

The guy sniffed at him, then turned and took a long whiff of Honey. Brayton knew the guy could smell how irritated he was, but he couldn't help himself.

"Doesn't smell that way to me."

"What!? Honey, what did you do?"

Truthfully, she looked as shocked as he felt, but he couldn't stay in that sardine-can any longer. He turned and shoved his way back out of the bus before his wolf-side went berserk.

"Brayton, wait!"

He didn't stop. He didn't want to hear anything she had to say. He couldn't. He was too busy trying to control his wolf.

20

Honey

"He seemed upset. Are you two a thing?" the troublemaker next to her inquired politely.

"No. What did you say your name was?"

"Daniel, Daniel Masterson." He stuck out his hand. "And you're Honey Smith, the best female MMA fighter I've ever had the pleasure to meet."

"Um, thank you." She shook his hand. It was large and rough and warm, but she didn't like touching him. There was something about him that rubbed her wrong. She went back to gazing out the window, hoping he'd get the hint.

"I'm sure he's fine," Daniel said.

"I'm sure he is too." She was actually jealous Brayton got to run on such a fine day. Maybe she should run too. The arena wasn't that far away from their hotel. In fact, she might be able to get there faster than the bus at the rate people were climbing on.

"What are you doing this evening?"

Apparently, he wasn't going to get the hint. She released an obvious sigh and turned to him. "I don't know. Could be anything from recovering from a broken bone to being unconscious to celebrating a victory."

"You're keeping your options open then?"

"I guess."

"Excellent. My evening is open too. If we both win, maybe we can celebrate together."

"Maybe. What if we're both unconscious?"

"Then we can celebrate that together too."

"Uh-huh."

He grinned and leaned close enough to whisper in her ear, "I like you Honey. I've been thinking of you ever since I met you."

That was understandable. She'd had a broken arm and there'd been some drama going on between her and bio-dad.

"Thank you?"

He chuckled. "I heard you used to be a rogue." He sniffed at her. "I don't smell a pack on you. Have you gone rogue again?"

"No." Her shield was too good. Phooey.

"Why can't I smell your pack?"

"Do I still smell like a wolf?"

"Yeah."

"Huh." The spell must consider the pack marks magical but not the smell of her wolf. Everyone was going to notice. She needed an excuse she could use without lying. "Well, I did visit an old building with a lot of magic. Maybe that had something to do with it."

"Really? Where was this old building?"

"Historical district."

"Why would visiting an old building affect your pack mark?" he asked skeptically.

She almost acted like she didn't know, but that would be a lie. She did know. She posed a question instead. "Why indeed?"

He chuckled. "A woman of mystery. I knew I liked you. Seriously though?"

"Seriously, it must remain a mystery."

"Honey, you made it. Where's Brayton?" Coach asked from the aisle.

"He went for a run."

"Ah, I guess he heard. The other guys made it so he won't be able to fight. I was hoping he'd be around to help you warm up though."

"I can help her, Sir," Daniel volunteered.

The coach looked Daniel up and down. "I'm sure your couch has his own plans. Honey, why don't you text Brayton and tell him to meet us there."

"Sure."

It was the first time she'd had a chance to look at her phone since her roommate had shaken her awake. To her surprise, there was a slew of texts from Brayton starting from ten last night. How had she slept through them all?

BB: (10:01 pm) We just landed. You still up?

BB: (10:15 pm) Guess you're asleep. See you in the morning.

BB: (6:00 am) Morning sunshine. Heard you got third yesterday. Good job.

BB: (6:05 am) Going downstairs to eat. See you there?

BB: (6:10 am) They have chocolate muffins!!!

BB: (6:15 am) You awake yet?

BB: (6:17 am) I know you're awake. You're always up before me. Come down. Please.

BB: (6:22 am) I guess this means you're still mad at me.

BB: (6:25 am) I miss talking to you.

BB: (6:31 am) Coach says get down here.

Anyone reading the messages would think they were good friends. She'd been ignoring the empty feeling in her chest since their fight, but his words reminded her it was there.

Me: I'm not mad. Coach says to meet us there.

Me: I'm still in your pack.

She wanted to tell him that as long as he didn't boss her friends around they'd get along fine, but she didn't want to start another argument.

What did he mean he missed talking to her? They didn't talk that much. She had been seeing a lot of him during MMA training, but that was just general chatting. It wasn't like the deep conversations she had with her friends during supper.

"I guess you got to walk along the Riverwalk since you were here yesterday. Did you ride a boat?" Daniel asked the second she put her phone away.

They chatted, well he talked, and she listened to his long-winded spiel about all the boats he'd been on the rest of the way to the arena.

21

Brayton

Several miles from the hotel, he slowed down and walked until he could breathe normally. Why was he so upset? He hadn't wanted Honey to be a part of his pack in the first place. He should just go back to ignoring her. It should be easier now at least.

He pulled out his phone and checked the time and his messages. There was one from Cici, two from Malcolm, one from Mom, and, his heart jumped, two from Honey. Eagerly, he touched her name. She was still in his pack and not mad at him! He felt lighter than he had all week. He needed to see her, to hug her, to feel they were all right. He googled how to get from where he was to her and started running.

His torso was slick with sweat when he reached his destination. He'd pulled off his shirt in time so it, at least, was dry and didn't smell. He stopped in a bathroom to wipe his pits and dab off the sweat, then jogged to the gym. The lovely aroma of old socks, sweat, musty gym mats, and a touch of angst greeted him well before he saw the doors.

A scrawny, pimply-faced guy with a squeaky voice stepped in front of the open door and stuck his hand out. "Stop. You cannot enter without a name tag or a bracelet."

"How do I get a name tag?"

Squeaky voice pointed to a table in the gym behind him where a bunch of people stood in line. "Over at the table."

"How can I get a name tag from that table if you're not letting me enter?"

"You have to go in the main door."

"How do I get there?"

"Go back down the hall, take a right, go all the way down that hall, take another right, and keep walking until you get to the end."

"Or you could just let me enter here and I'll walk directly to the table."

"I can't let you do that. Everyone has to enter through the main door. It's the rule."

Brayton was very tempted to go alpha on the squirt.

"Brayton! I've got your name tag."

There were people everywhere, but all he could focus on was Honey jogging toward him with a smile, for him. She probably wasn't planning to hug him, but as soon as she was close enough, he grabbed her and pulled her close. She hugged him back and actually relaxed against him a little. He buried his nose in her hair and took a deep breath. Still pack, still Honey, still his.

"Excuse me, Honey," squeaky voice said. "You dropped this." He held out a black hair-thingy.

Honey stepped out of Brayton's arms to take it and Brayton forced himself to stifle his growl.

"Thank you, Jasper. He has his name tag now," she handed Brayton a lanyard with the all-important name tag at the end. "Will you let him in now?"

"He's supposed to go through the main door."

"The ladies at the table gave us his lanyard. If they'd wanted him to go through the front they wouldn't have."

Jasper looked at the table and then back at Brayton as if he was actually considering sending him through the main door.

"My match starts in twenty minutes. He's supposed to help me warm up. Will you please let him in?"

Jasper let out the longest sigh Brayton had ever heard. "I suppose, but only for you, Honey." He fluttered his eyelashes at her. The guy had ridiculously long eyelashes – almost as ridiculous as Tuula's.

"Thank you, Jasper."

The sincerity of the smile Honey bestowed on the pipsqueak almost made Brayton jealous, which was ludicrous. He shook it off and put the lanyard over his head, then stepped into the sacred gym. Jasper didn't even notice. He was too busy waving at Honey who was already bounding back to the mats.

Honey was marvelous. Brayton missed not being able to compete himself but watching her was almost as fun and it gave him an advantage over all the other guys trying to vie for her attention. Jerk-face kept coming by to congratulate her but he had his own matches to get ready for so he couldn't stay long. Deacon was in the stands close to where Honey was resting between matches, but he wasn't allowed on the floor. Brayton was surprised Damien didn't come down to throw his weight around or offer advice. He'd made it to nationals a couple of times, but he stayed several rows up next to his dad. The few times Brayton glanced up that way, he looked bored.

Mom, Bernadette, Cici, and Liam were sitting at about the same level as Alpha Meyer, but in the next section over. His mom always cheered for people, but her cheers were at the level of the rest of the crowd. Bernadette and Cici were taking it a level above with chest bumps, foam hands, and a poster of a beehive that said 'Touch our Honey, Feel the Sting'. Alpha Silver and his wife joined the group after Honey had won her first two matches. By the time it got down to the final match, the whole section was chanting Honey's name.

Honey smiled and waved at them, but when she turned her back on them to focus on the mats, her face was tense and she smelled worried and nervous. Brayton would be concerned too. The last girl Honey had to fight had won the past two years and her dad was a famous fighter from California. Coach Peters started muttering in Honey's ear. Brayton knew from experience coach was going over her competitor's strengths and weaknesses. Brayton moved closer to stand on her other side.

"The fight for the women's national title will begin in five minutes. That's five minutes, folks. Senior and two-time champion Stacia Rowland from Clearlake University, California will take on Freshman Honey Smith from Vindale University, Indiana. The final men's match will take place immediately after," a voice boomed over the loudspeakers.

Whatever the coach was whispering wasn't making Honey any less tense.

Brayton waited for the coach to finish, then muttered, "You're going to lose."

Honey looked at him in shock. "What!"

"And you know what? I don't care. None of those people in the stands will think any less of you either. I think, for a rogue, you've done marvelous. Of course, knowing you, you'll probably go out and give like 150% and pull out some new move no one has ever seen before and make her do a face plant into the mat, just to prove me wrong. Anyone else in your place would be nervous and intimidated, but you? You're so stubborn you're going to go out there and have fun trying to figure out how to knock her over because you like a challenge. And when she tries to psych you out with her words and her fists, you'll ignore the fact that she's bigger and stronger than you and sting her in the ass like the smart little wasp you are."

"Wasp?"

He shrugged. "Bees lose their stingers. I'd rather you keep yours."

She gave him a crooked grin the made his heart happy. "I think that's your best pep-talk yet."

"Thanks." He put his arm around her. The more time he spent around her, the harder it was to keep from touching her. He couldn't deny it anymore. It wasn't only fate that made him long to be close to her. "Just go out there and have fun, okay." He made a fist and rubbed his knuckles against the top of her head to keep himself from kissing her. "Use that wacky brain of yours to bring her down."

She pulled away from him and smoothed down her hair. "A brain laser would be nice about now."

"How would that even work?"

She put two fingers in front of her eyes and jabbed them forward. "Through my eyes, like superman."

"That would be illegal," he declared in his best lawyer-like voice.

"Spoilsport."

"Get out there, Honey," the Coach said. "Show her how it's done."

"And have fun!" Brayton called.

Stacia had long, straight dark-hair and stood about the same height as Honey, but while Honey was lithe, Stacia was buff. They shook hands and said something to each other, but Honey's smile was painted on so he couldn't tell if Stacia said something rude or polite.

Stacia attacked as soon as the ref said 'Begin'. Honey glided out of the way, and managed a block when Stacia threw a sneak punch. Honey retaliated with a sneaky kick that didn't do much physically but had to mentally concern the other girl. Stacia attacked again. Honey evaded and landed a fist between the other girl's shoulders. Again, not much physically, but he got a good look at Stacia's face when she turned around to face Honey again. She was pissed.

He felt a weak trickle of alpha power from the direction of the mat. It was so weak, most wolves probably wouldn't realize it was there. He only did because it made his power want to fight back. Someone was trying to cheat. He could have located the source by letting his own power feel it out, but he didn't want Honey to be accused of cheating herself. Whoever it was, was either trying to influence Honey or influence the judges, or maybe they were just excited.

The power grew. The one alpha judge didn't call anything so the judges must not be the targets. That meant Honey must be the target. He snorted to himself. She was in the process of irritating another alpha and didn't even realize it.

Stacia wasn't looking so good. Her face was starting to shine with perspiration and she was panting. She'd tried multiple attacks, but each time, Honey avoided and countered with minimal movement, then grinned. Stacia growled and threw herself at Honey again. He expected Honey to suddenly go on the offensive like she tended to do, but she just sidestepped Stacia again and threw another fist into her back as she passed. Stacia abruptly spun and tried to grab Honey's middle. Honey jumped up and over so that her hands were on Stacia's shoulders, then did a kind of flip to her feet. Stacia stumbled forward from the weight and then face-planted into the mat when Honey spun to kick Stacia in the rear just before the first round was called.

Honey bounced off the mat and grabbed the water bottle he was holding. "How was that? Did you like my move?"

He thought it was excellent, but he wobbled his hand back and forth as if it was only so-so. "Eh."

She narrowed her eyes at him. "You got your face plant though."

"Yes, yes, I did. I bow to your marvelousness." He bowed.

"And the rear sting."

"Ah yes, that too." He bowed again.

"What are you doing Brayton? You look like one of those pop-up clowns," Coach said. "Honey, you need to be more aggressive. If you hadn't worked that last move in at the last second, she might have won the round."

"Yes, Coach."

"Also, someone was trying to influence you with alpha power. Any idea who?" Brayton asked.

"I thought Stacia looked bigger," Honey commented like a woman having alpha power was normal.

"Are you sure?" he asked.

Honey shrugged.

"That's cheating!" Coach said. "Do you know what this means?"

"It means she's going to have an ugly wake-up call. Honey is immune to alpha power," Brayton informed him.

"What?" Coach looked from Brayton to Honey with wide eyes.

"Yeah, it surprised me too," Brayton said, "and is really irritating. Usually. Let them fight."

Honey flashed a toothy grin.

Coach nodded. "Okay, get out there. Stop being so nice."

"Yes, Coach."

He felt the power again just before the round started. Stacia hissed at Honey to stand still. Five seconds after the round started, Honey landed a spinning head kick and knocked Stacia out cold. The alpha power he felt abruptly cut off. The strength of the cheers that erupted behind him was actually scary. Honey wasn't phased though. She turned to the crowd and raised both arms with the biggest grin he'd ever seen her wear. And then he might have gotten a little carried away. He wasn't sure later how he got from where he was to the middle of the mat, but he picked her up and squeezed her in a spinning hug right there in front of everyone.

"Brayton, you can put me down now." She whacked his shoulders with her fists. "Brayton!"

He dropped her. "Sorry."

She laughed and his heart sang.

Someone brought out a trophy that looked like an MMA belt with a wolf face and fist coming toward the viewer. Subtle. Honey accepted her award, but then handed it off to the coach to go speak with Stacia, who was conscious again.

Stacia slapped Honey's hand away and scowled at her. No surprise there.

"What did you say?" he asked when Honey joined them at their seats.

"It was nice fighting with you."

"You didn't mention…"

"Nope. Didn't see the point. I'll let her wonder."

Her eyes were alive with happiness and she glowed with excitement. She was a little sweaty from all the fighting, but it only served to make her amazing scent even stronger. He really, really wanted to ….

Jerk-face landed abruptly next to them from where he'd jumped over the railing on the front of the stands. Show off. "Honey, that was excellent."

"Thank you."

"About our date tonight."

His heart stopped at the same time his wolf decided it was time to come out.

"You said if we both won," Honey said, and pointedly opened her palm toward the two guys getting ready to face off for the final fight, neither of which was jerk-face.

"Besides, my Luna is here and I'm sure she already has plans. Brayton, are you okay? Your face is all red."

Grabbing his chest wasn't really helping him not to shift. "Yes." He sounded like an old frog. "Just need a drink." He turned away and worked on breathing while squirting water in him face.

"Having trouble Brayton?" Cici smirked down at him from the front row of the bleachers.

"Shut-up Cici."

"Your mom said to tell you she'll meet you guys at the hotel after Honey's had a chance to clean up. She's invited Alpha Silver and his wife and Liam out to dinner. She said for Honey to invite your coach. I'm sure your mom wouldn't mind if Honey invited that hot guy too."

"I don't know who you are talking about."

Cici snickered and turned to go back up in the stands.

Deacon stopped Cici at the end of the row. "Where are you guys going?"

"I don't know. You'll have to ask Luna Lynn," Cici said.

22

Honey

The blue dress would have been perfect to wear to the fancy restaurant Luna Lynn was taking them to if it wasn't all crumpled and didn't smell like herbs. Her only other option was some tight black pants and a sleeveless black shirt. The shirt had a pretty collar at least. Lynn rented a car, but the restaurant wasn't far from the hotel, so Liam, Cici, Brayton, and Honey walked. Cici had flown down with Luna Lynn and Bernadette specifically to watch Honey fight, or so she said.

Bio-dad was waiting outside the restaurant with a petite woman with dark blond, wavy hair. The blond woman had packed appropriately. Her frilly dress was perfect for the weather and the restaurant. Bio-dad gave Honey a hug, then indicated the woman.

"Honey, this is Tanya, my wife. Tanya, this is Honey."

Honey had thought it would be strange meeting the woman who'd taken her mother's place by bio-dad's side, but it was just like meeting any other person. "Hello."

Tanya clasped Honey's hand in both of hers. "Hello. Rory has told me so much about you. I'm glad to finally meet you. That was some awesome fighting today, by the way. Congratulations."

"Thank you."

"Rory said Matt put you in lessons at the age of three?"

"Yes."

"It shows."

Tanya beamed at her. Honey gave another lame thank you and tried to beam back.

Lynn provided Honey an excuse to retrieve her hand by appearing with Bernadette, Coach Peters, Alpha Meyer, his two sons, and a plump woman with a diminutive posture that Honey had never met before. Lynn gestured toward the unknown woman.

"Honey, this is Luna Meyer."

The woman lifted her head and looked so worn and sad Honey immediately felt the need to comfort her. She stuck her hand out. "Hello. It's nice to meet you."

The woman didn't take it. She gave a little nod and looked down again. "Likewise."

"Looks like we're all here. Shall we go in?" Lynn asked smoothly.

The restaurant had a Tex-Mex, rich rancher style. The waitress led them to a long, heavy wooden table in a private alcove with dark wooden beams and wrought-iron chandeliers overhead and a huge stone fireplace with a thick wooden mantle at one end. There wasn't a fire though. The adults clustered around the end of the table near the fireplace. Luna Meyer sat between her husband and Damien. Honey and her friends took over the other end. It was the first time Honey had been close to Damien since he'd been ill. The change was dramatic. He'd lost weight and barely lifted his head. She saw his mother talking to him occasionally, but her voice was so soft and the others so loud, Honey couldn't hear anything Luna Meyer said.

Everyone else was in a great mood. Brayton described the earlier matches her bio-dad hadn't been able to see, then started going over the ones he had. From the excitement in his voice, it sounded like he was talking about a pro-fighter. Deacon jumped in and started talking about some of the other fights, which was more than fine with her. She hadn't been able to see much from their seats and she'd been busy with her own matches. Damien never said a word. She hadn't liked the way he acted before but seeing him so down bothered her, and she could still smell the spell. It seemed stronger when she walked past him on her way to the bathroom. Hadn't his brother told him it was a spell? Why hadn't Damien had it removed? She pushed back from the table when everyone was chatting while they waited for dessert, walked around to Damien, and leaned down next to his ear.

"Will you walk with me for a moment? There's something you need to know."

He shook his head. "Leave me alone."

His mother heard, but she looked worried instead of mad when she glanced up at Honey.

Honey tried again. "I figured out what that smell is," she said as quietly as she could. "It's a spell. Someone has put a spell on you. Come with me for a few minutes so I can figure out where it is."

"What!" He spun his head around to look her and scooted his chair back with an awful screeching noise. His scary self was still in there.

The rest of the table looked up at them in alarm.

Honey lifted her hands, palms up to indicate everyone should stay where they were. "It's okay. I startled him. Go back to your conversation."

Damien grabbed her elbow. His eyes were both desperate and angry. "Honey?"

She jerked her arm away. "Let's talk on the balcony."

Lynn frowned and opened her mouth, probably to object, but Brayton jumped in. "I'll go too. I need some fresh air."

The balcony was right outside the room and extended all the way across the building with a great view of the Riverwalk. Below them, colorful umbrellas shielded diners from their view and a boat full of tourists floated slowly by.

As soon as the door shut, Damien grabbed her shoulder and spun her around. "What do you mean I've been spelled?"

"Hey, hands off," Brayton demanded, stepping forward to interfere.

To her surprise, Damien not only released her, he stepped back and hung his head. "Sorry. I haven't been myself lately."

"We heard you were ill."

Damien sighed and lifted his head. "Tell me what you wanted to say."

"That smell is a spell. Sorry it took me so long to realize." She sniffed and wished she hadn't. "It smells like deceit and pain and dust...vacuum cleaner dust," she abruptly realized.

"What does that mean?" he demanded.

203

"Someone is tricking you and sucking something from you?" she guessed. "Are you wearing anything that someone has given you recently? Something that they gave to your brother or that you loaned him because I have smelled it on him too but not all the time."

His eyes dropped immediately to the phone watch on his arm.

"Take it off and put it on the ground for a moment and step away. If that's it, the smell should stay."

He did as she asked. She walked around him then toward the watch. "Yep. That's it."

Damien growled and punched the brick wall, hard. She suspected he broke his hand, but he didn't act like it hurt.

"What do I do? How do I break it?"

She wasn't about to try and break it in front of him. She had her hair-band on her wrist but she didn't know how well it would hide the smell of magic if she actively tried to do some.

"You should take it to a witch. Find out what it was for."

"Oh, I know what it was for. It's to take my alpha power."

"What!?" Brayton said in shock. "They can do that?"

Honey squatted down and looked at the watch with her magic sight. The molecules looked fine, so she looked even deeper. The back of the watch looked strange. She turned it on its side. One side, the side that would be in contact with Damien's skin, swirled with orange.

"What are you doing?" Damien asked. "You probably shouldn't touch it."

"I think the spell is just on the back of the watch part. Does your power come back if you stop wearing it?"

"No."

She picked the watch up by the band and took another sniff. Nasty. The smells of deceit and pain were extremely unpleasant, kind of like she imagined standing in a sewer would be. She turned her head away to take a fresh breath before she chucked up all the Mexican food she'd just eaten. She did catch something else this time though. It was faint, but it reminded her of the tire swing that one of the houses she'd lived in had out back. Her dad had replaced the old, frayed rope with a new one, and then ended up replacing the tire too. She'd loved that swing.

"Rope. I smell rope. Your power has been bound."

"It's still there?" Damien asked hopefully.

"I don't know. I'm guessing. I don't think it's possible to completely take a power, unless you physically damage the part of you that is responsible for making it. It's like memories. You can magically erase memories or use a spell to keep them from forming, but the ability to remember is still there, I think." She really had no idea, but it made sense.

"How do you know so much about spells?"

"I don't. I'm using logic."

"Magic isn't logical."

She didn't argue. There was no point.

"If it's a spell, how come Deacon still has his power?" Damian challenged.

"I don't know. Maybe it's tailored to you."

"We're identical!"

"Genetically, but I can tell you apart. Maybe spells are the same way. I don't know. You need to ask a witch."

"Who would you recommend?"

"Someone on the witch council?" she could ask her friends to recommend someone, but he'd be more likely to find a witch that would work with him if the Council directed him, she assumed.

"What about your friends?"

"Don't you already know a witch," Brayton interrupted. "Why don't you ask the one who sold you that necklace you tried to spell Honey with."

"She refused to help," Damien said in disgust.

"She probably didn't have the right kind of magic," Honey supplied. "None of my friends do either except maybe Daegal, but he's still learning. This is beyond him."

"Just go to the Council," Brayton said.

Damian shook his big head. "I don't want the Council involved, not yet. They always drag their feet and make excuses. Anyone else?"

She hesitated too long.

"Who?" he demanded.

"There's one person. She might be able to give you more information on spells, but she doesn't like wolves and we've… had a few disagreements, so you cannot tell her I mentioned her. Don't even hint. Especially don't tell her that it was a wolf who told you because she'll know it was me. Oh, and you have to be super polite or she'll probably spell you or shock you or something."

"Where do I find her?" Damien demanded.

She shouldn't have said anything. "Seriously Damien, you cannot offend her. You have to treat her like a queen and don't make demands or she won't help you at all."

"Okay, I get it. Just tell me where to find her."

There was no way she was telling him in front of Brayton. She pulled out her phone and handed it to him. "Put your number in. I'll text you the information."

The door opened and Bio-dad stuck out his head. "Dessert is here."

"We were just coming in." She handed the watch to Damien and waited for him to go ahead of her.

"It's nice out here." Bio-dad stepped out and to the side so Damien could pass him. He watched Damien until he had reached the table inside, then turned and said in a low voice to Brayton. "I'd like a moment alone with Honey."

"Sure."

Bio-dad indicated she should step to the side where nobody could see them through the window, then pulled her into a tight hug.

"I am so proud of you! I'm sure Matt and your mom would have been too."

"I know."

He sniffed, then held her out at arm's length. "Honey, has something happened? Why can't I smell a pack mark on you?"

She couldn't help grinning as she rolled the hairband off her wrist and handed it to him. "Smell now."

He did, then held up the hairband. "What is this?"

She took it from him and slipped it back on. "My first spell. Two, actually. Mom's family found out my name and were using a tracking spell to find me, then they scried me too. I found a spell to block them from seeing me, then I used the same spell to block people from smelling magic. The only problem is, pack marks are magic too. I'm going to try and tweak it when I get back to make it work better."

"That's your first spell? You've never done others?"

She shrugged. "Mom's magic was a lot different than mine. She taught me what she could, but she couldn't acquire magical books without risking discovery."

"What about her friends?"

"We moved so much she didn't have many, and the ones she did talk to were all human."

"Ah." He turned to look out over the balcony. "Do you know how they discovered your name?"

"No." The librarian could have told them, but Honey wasn't going to ask.

"You better get back inside. I think they brought you fried ice cream."

"Okay."

23

Honey

Everyone flew back on Sunday. She spent Sunday night in the boys' suite but moved back to her room on Monday since no one had come looking for her and it was challenging to get ready for school in a dorm full of boys.

Random wolves congratulated her on her win all day. A lot of them were upperclassmen she'd never met before. Several guys invited her to spar in the gym sometime. She told them she would when she had the chance.

Since nobody came for her the rest of the week, she assumed her shield spells were working. Just in case, she ate a purple radish every morning. She also stayed away from other wolves so they wouldn't notice her pack mark was missing. She wasn't quite sure how to fix that and there wasn't anyone she could ask.

She'd never found time during her trip to read the book the librarian had given her. The only place truly safe for her to read it was her room. She started reading a few chapters every day. By Thursday, she was past a general description of blood curses and was now into descriptions of real ones. So far, only one had been broken but that was because the one who did the cursing removed it when his wife came back.

Reading about the curses and probably the fact that she had to hide to do it, made her a little jumpy, so when someone pounded on the door, she jumped like a startled cat.

"Who is it?"

"Why don't you turn on your phone and see," Brayton's voice came through the door.

She hid the book under her covers and hopped down off her bunk. She sniffed, but she'd been exposed to the magical scent coming off the book too long to tell how bad it was. Hopefully, between the open window and the residual magic in the dorm, Brayton wouldn't be able to smell anything.

"How are you here?" she asked when she opened the door. "Boys can't be here without an escort."

He jerked his thumb down the hall. "Cici. She had to go."

"What do you need?"

"Mom's looking for you. What did you do, Honey?"

"What do you mean?"

"There's an investigator with her from Texas."

"I didn't do anything."

He sighed while she wracked her brain trying to figure out why an investigator would want to talk to her. Sure, she'd visited a witch university, but that wasn't illegal, and she may have used magic on a witch, but that was in self-defense. Had the witches figured out she was a wolch? Should she run? Where would she go? She didn't want to leave her friends.

Brayton touched her arm, then slid his hand down to take hers. "Come on. I'll go with you."

For a moment she thought he meant he'd run away with her. Strangely, she didn't mind the idea at all.

"Why are you looking at me like that?"

She came to her senses. "Hold on." She slipped her hand out of his and grabbed her backpack. If she had to freeze someone and run, she at least wanted the cash cards and the change of clothes she always carried with her.

Lynn and a tan man of medium height and build and a big belt buckle were waiting in front of her dorm. Lynn shot her a concerned look, then pulled up a polite smile and introduced him.

"Honey, this is detective Saulnier from San Antonio. He'd like to ask you a few questions about a theft."

That wasn't what she'd been expecting. She felt light with relief. "A theft?"

His nose twitched and she wondered if he could smell the magic from the book on her hands. It would be nice if she could test her anti-magic shield more thoroughly. She should ask the boys to tell her if they could smell anything next time she saw them. The detective stepped so that he was downwind of her, probably to detect lies. He was likely wondering why he couldn't detect her pack mark. Too bad. She wasn't about to take off her spelled hair tie.

"What was stolen?" she asked.

"I'll ask the questions," the guy snapped.

"Maybe we should do this somewhere more private," Lynn suggested sweetly. "I'm sure we can find an empty meeting room in the Admin building."

"Fine. Lead the way," the detective said. He indicated Honey should go ahead of him. Brayton followed all the way to the door of the room but the detective refused to let him in. He tried to keep Lynn from going in too, but she explained that Honey was a minor and her ward and that by law he couldn't question Honey without her present, then gave him a very polite, yet steely smile. He caved.

It felt like an interrogation room the way he pointed to a wooden chair and made her sit, then plopped down in the rolling office chair across the table. He leaned forward so his elbows and lower arms were on the hard surface and stared her right in the eyes.

"Did you or did you not visit the Opal Lambert House Museum last Friday around 2 p.m.?"

How was she supposed to answer that? "Yes?"

"You admit you visited it?" He sounded surprised.

"Um no. You asked if I did or did not visit it. The answer to that is yes, I did do one of those two things."

"Why are teenagers always such smart-asses?"

Did he really want her to answer that? "Umm, is it because we haven't yet learned all we don't know or because our youth makes us feel invincible?"

He slapped his hand down on the table hard enough to make her jump. "Do you know what the punishment is for stealing?"

"No. I assume it depends on what was stolen."

He pulled a picture out of his breast pocket and laid it firmly on the desk in front of her. "This."

It was an extremely large, gaudy gold pendant on a thick chain with an amber jewel in the middle and gold rays shooting from it like it was the sun. "Why would someone steal that?"

"Because it's priceless."

"What does it do?"

He narrowed his eyes at her. "Why did you ask that?"

"Because it's so ugly no one would want it unless it was magical."

Lynn made a sound like a snort, then acted like she was clearing her throat.

"Did you take this?" the detective asked.

"No. I've never seen it before."

"You were seen going into the museum right before the time someone noticed it was gone."

"No I wasn't."

"There are witnesses."

"Well, they didn't see what they thought they saw then because I didn't go into the museum."

He pulled out another picture and put it in front of her. She was wearing the blue dress and hair. "Is this you?"

She pulled at one of her brown strands. "Do I look like I have blue hair?"

"Don't play dumb. I know it's you. There are cameras everywhere. We saw a girl in blue go into the bathroom and never come out, but you did yet you never went in." He laid down another picture of her standing with Liam. Liam had his arm around her shoulder.

"Maybe she used a portal," Honey suggested.

"What do you know about portals?"

"Nothing. I'm just saying, there are other possible explanations."

The grumpy man slammed his fist down on the table. "I know it's you. Facial recognition software isn't fooled by hair."

She knew she should just answer his questions, but she hadn't done anything wrong. She shrugged. "Even if it is me, I didn't go into any museums."

"Why were you dressed like that then?"

"Surely you know what the museum really is. The place reeks of magic."

"You could smell it?"

"Yeah. Can't you?" She was pretty sure Liam had been able to smell it, although he hadn't said as much now that she thought about it.

"What is it?" Luna asked.

The detective didn't answer. Did he really not know what it was?

"The museum sign is fake," she told Lynn. "The building is actually a college for witches."

"Is the girl in blue you, Honey?" Luna Lynn asked.

She didn't mind answering Lynn. "Yes."

"Did you go into the school?"

"Yes."

"Did you steal the necklace?" Lynn's voice was carefully neutral, but Honey could still hear the hurt.

"No."

"Why did you enter then?"

"I heard they had a magical library. I wanted to see it. I went in, looked in a book, and went out. There was no necklace. They did get a little mad. Someone sent out a message to all the students to look for someone with blue hair. I'm guessing they got the police involved because they couldn't access all the cameras at the restaurants."

Honey looked pointedly at the detective. "They're using you to find me."

"Honey, what were you thinking? We're trying to improve relations to the witches, not make them mad," Lynn said. Now she sounded disappointed, but there was a hint of relief too.

"They didn't know I was a wolf."

"Honey, witches can always tell."

Honey shook her head. "Nope. There are ways to hide it and they work well when you're surrounded by a lot of magic."

"Did Liam know what you were up to?"

"Yeah, but neither of us knew exactly what we were getting into."

"And here I thought that boy had a good head on his shoulders."

"He does." She was afraid to say anything else in case they interviewed him. She wanted their stories to match.

"If they thought you were a witch, why did they get mad?"

Now the detective got smart.

"Because they took my blood without my permission. I didn't want them to know what I was so I destroyed their tester. Don't worry," she said when Lynn opened her mouth, "I don't think it was expensive. It looked like a big guitar pick and it was made of plastic."

"How did you make it through the wards and what was it like inside?" the inspector asked.

"I walked in and it looked just like it does outside the ward but with people around."

"You just walked through their wards?"

"Yep." She grinned like she was hiding something, because she was, but not what he was hopefully assuming

215

– that she had a charm. "I have a lot of friends who are witches," she said to get him leaning that way.

"What about inside. What did you see?"

"A hallway and the library. The library was nice. It has floor to ceiling books and some comfy chairs. I think there was a fireplace too."

"Did you talk to anyone?"

"Yes, the future owner of the school and her great-something aunt who used to be a person but is now a, I guess, guardian spell?"

"What was the aunt's name?"

"Philomena."

The inspector took a deep breath, probably to check for lies, then leaned back and huffed. "She's the one who reported the necklace stolen. Those liars." He shook his finger at Honey, "although you shouldn't have been trespassing."

She disagreed. She had as much right to be there as any other witch but she couldn't tell him that. "Please don't tell them my name or that I am wolf. I don't want to cause any trouble between the witches and the wolves."

"You should have considered that in the first place."

"Why do you think I wore a disguise?"

He leaned forward. "You tell me where you got that charm to get through their wards and I'll consider not giving out your name."

"That's enough. She answered the relevant questions," Lynn snapped. "She is innocent of a crime that was never committed. For the sake of peace, it would be best if anything tying the girl in blue to Honey would disappear."

"I have to file a report and explain why I flew all the way here."

"Just tell the truth," Lynn said. "The girl you identified in the photos didn't steal anything. You guys follow false leads all the time, don't you."

"Yeah, but I usually don't fly to another state."

"You could have just had a local inspector come talk to her, but you were hoping you'd get some recognition because she was associated with three alphas, am I right?" Lynn asked sagely. "They caught a picture of you with us at that Mexican restaurant," Lynn explained before Honey could ask.

The inspector's face looked like it was chiseled out of stone.

"Did you ask to see where the necklace was in the museum or investigate the premises at all?" Lynn asked. "For that matter, is there even a museum?"

"No, but they'd never admit that and they'd never let us into the school."

"Then you can't be expected to solve the case."

Lynn got up and abruptly opened the door. Brayton fell inside.

"Brayton," Luna said, as if he wasn't picking himself up from the floor, "take the detective to his car. Honey and I need to have a little chat."

Lynn shut the door after they left, opened it and looked both ways, then shut it again before she sat down in front of Honey.

"Poor Brayton. These doors are too thick to listen through. Now tell me what's going on Honey."

"What?"

"I know you didn't just break into a magical library on a whim."

"What if I did?"

She crossed her arms. "Then I would be very disappointed in you. Besides, I doubt Liam would help you unless there was a very good reason. From what I've seen, he's a very responsible young man."

Honey couldn't tell Lynn she was a wolch, so she told her about the cursed land and how she was trying to find a way to break the curse. It was true, just not why she was in the Texas library.

"That Zavier," Lynn sighed when Honey was done. "He should have known better than to ask you to help him. Grown witches haven't been able to break that curse and you're just a pup."

"The witches thought it was animal blood. I found the human body that was used. Well, what's left of it. I can smell where the boundaries are. That's information the witches didn't have. If I can find something similar in a book, maybe it will have the answer."

Lynn shook her head. "You are a sweet child Honey. No more sneaking into magical libraries though, okay?"

She couldn't promise that. "How will I find out about the curse then? Besides, do you know where another library exists? I think the witches hide them."

"Honey."

"Fine, I won't try to sneak past any librarians."

Lynn narrowed her eyes at Honey. "Mmm. And why can't I smell your pack mark?"

Should she tell her about the hairband? Lynn hadn't said anything about the supposed charm she'd used to get through the witch's wards. Maybe she wouldn't care. "Because I'm wearing a shield charm," Honey said slowly.

"And why is that?"

"So the witches can't scry me or locate me." She didn't mention which witches.

Lynn snorted. "Smart. Better keep it on for a while.

24

Brayton

The man didn't look happy. "Did you find out what you needed?" Brayton asked the detective.

"Tell me about Honey."

Like he would say anything about a pack member. "What do you want to know?"

"Is she a troublemaker?"

Brayton laughed. He couldn't help it.

"She ever been arrested before?"

That didn't help. Brayton had to take several deep breaths before he could answer. "No."

"Would you say she has an unnatural obsession with witches?"

He snorted.

"So, she does?"

"That depends on your point of view."

"What do you mean?"

He shook his head. He'd said too much already.

"Tell me this then, would you be surprised to hear that she walked right into a college full of witches just to look at a book because she was curious?"

"Is that what she did?"

"That's what she claims."

He recalled the time Honey had sequestered herself in the library for hours just to finish a book and then remembered the librarian who'd been looking for her in the Union. Had the librarian been mad because Honey snuck into a section she wasn't supposed to see?

"No, I wouldn't be surprised at all. Honey loves books. She's really smart too. She got a perfect score on her SAT."

"She did, did she," the man mumbled under his breath.

"Did you hear she won the MMA championship at the Games?"

"I heard a freshman won. That was her."

"Yep."

The man sighed, then brightened.

"No. She didn't use magic," Brayton informed him before the man could finish forming the thought. "I was right there. I would have smelled it. Besides, I've practiced with her for months. She really is that good, as I'm sure our coach would attest."

Brayton didn't take the man all the way to his car. He pointed the way to the parking lot and turned back. Mom and Honey were just coming down the stairs when he reached the Admin building.

"Brayton, good. I want you to assign people in the pack to escort Honey between classes for a few weeks," Mom said.

"You don't need to do that. The boys already are." Honey said.

"Why? What's wrong?" he demanded.

221

"Honey stirred up a nest of witches down in Texas. I've heard they are particularly venomous down there, and I don't mean that in a bad way," his mom quickly added. "Just that they are dangerous to cross, even if it is only a perceived slight."

Honey's shoulders sagged. "I'm sorry. I didn't mean to cause any problems."

Mom put her arm over Honey's shoulders. "I know dear. You were only trying to help."

"Help what?" he asked.

Mom glanced at her watch. "Honey can tell you. I have to go."

His mom went back upstairs. He stayed with Honey.

"Okay, what's going on?" he asked as soon as they were outside.

She turned away from him and started walking down the sidewalk.

Not again. He jogged forward and grabbed her hand. "Honey, please don't walk away from me. I don't want to fight with you again. I only want to help you."

She stopped but she didn't look up. "I know Brayton."

He stepped closer and used a piece of hair as an excuse to touch her. The strand curled around his finger like a little vine. "Talk to me Honey. Who were you trying to help?"

"Zavier, but one thing led to another and, no. That's not right. If I hadn't...no, that would have happened anyway and I would have had no warning." She looked up at him with her amazing eyes as full as they could possibly be with tears. "I'm so tired of hiding, Brayton. Why can't I just be myself?"

He pulled her to his chest. "You can always be yourself with me. Always."

She pushed away, shaking her head. "I wish I could, Brayton. I wish with all my heart that I could."

What more was she was hiding? He grabbed her hand when she tried to walk away from him, again. "Honey, I know you have an unnatural affinity for witches and that you're amazingly smart and stubborn and a great fighter. I accept all that and if there's more, I accept that too. There's nothing you could say that would make me dislike you."

She looked back over her shoulder. "What if I told you I was your sister?"

"What!?" His heart did a strange free-fall in his chest.

"Kidding."

She pulled her hand free and continued back toward her dorm. He jogged up to her side.

"Hey, I know something that will make you feel better."

"What?"

"We can go to the gym. I'll let you beat me a few times."

She raised an eyebrow. "You'll let me?"

"Yeah, because that's the kind of friend I am."

From her doubtful look, he knew she was going to say no before she opened her mouth. It took him a few moments to realized what she'd actually said.

"Wait, what?"

She grinned at him. "I said okay."

25

Honey

Between studying and being escorted everywhere and Honey's inability to tell Brayton no whenever he begged her to go to the gym with him, meaning she was rarely alone, it took another week to finish the book. She'd learned a few things, but she still didn't know how to break the curse.

She hadn't stepped foot in the library since the librarian had tried to take her blood and she had no plans to, but she didn't want the librarian to think she'd stolen the book.

"Blaze, can you drop magical books in the regular library drop box?"

"It's not encouraged. Did you finally finish that thing?"

Her roommate knew about the book and that something had happened between the librarian and her, but she didn't know what.

"Yeah."

"I can take it back for you."

"I wish I could ask for another one, but with only four weeks left of school, I probably won't have time to read it."

Blaze snorted. "Please. I've never seen anyone read as fast as you can. The only reason it took you so long this time was because of a certain alpha-to-be."

"That's not true."

Blaze raised her eyebrows. "Are you kidding me? Brayton is following you around like a little puppy. He's even changed tables in the cafeteria. The only time you aren't with him is when you're here."

"No. I spend plenty of time without him. You just notice because he's been eating with us and he's only doing that because his mom asked him to keep an eye on me in case those Texas witches show up."

"Uh huh."

"If Brayton is a puppy, how would you classify Panas?" Honey asked evilly. "Ever since that match…"

"I take it all back," Blaze said, her cheeks turning pink. "Brayton is clearly just a friend. Moving on… We can check books out over the summer you know."

Honey didn't understand why Blaze was all but ignoring Panas lately even though the boy was doing all he could to get her attention, but it wasn't really any of her business.

"The only reason the librarian let me check this one out was because she didn't want to get caught with a wolf in the library. Besides, I don't want to remind her that you're my friend. If you ask for the next book in the series, she'll know."

"What about the witch who cast the spell? What was his name?"

"Witthem."

"I'll see if I can find something on him. Wouldn't it be great if his Grimoire somehow ended up in the library?"

"Mmm, well…"

Blaze laughed. "Don't worry. Grimoires of evil witches are typically not found in common libraries. They keep them locked up at the council library."

"Why do they keep them at all?"

"In case they need to undo a spell like this one."

Mr. Witthem probably *had* written the curse down since it took so long to develop. "Is there a way to find out if is being stored somewhere?"

"Maybe. I could ask the librarian. I'll say I'm researching a possible topic for my future thesis," she said when Honey started to protest.

"Thesis?" Honey asked.

"Yeah. All the witches enrolled in the college of magic have to write one to graduate."

Honey wondered what her mother had written about. She was sure her mom had been enrolled even though the only degrees her mom had ever told her about were math and business.

"See if there's any information on Witthem's wife. I suspect he used her blood and buried her on the property."

"That's despicable."

"I know, right. It would be more than fitting if I did find a way to break the curse and Zavier was able to use the land to help women and children."

"You know," Blaze said thoughtfully. "If she was treated like the women your friend Zavier is trying to help and sacrificed unwillingly, it might help."

"What do you mean?"

"Magic is about intent. The man who instituted the curse wanted to protect his family and his heritage. Now, if the woman was dying anyway, she might have agreed to let him use her blood. Her intent would also be protection. However, if she was murdered and supplied her blood unwillingly, her intent might be revenge or it might be to get away, but it won't be protection, which means the spell isn't as strong as it could be."

"How does that help?"

"It doesn't really, unless you can find a way to explain to her remaining essence what you wish to do and she agrees. Since it's her blood that powered the spell, she ultimately has a say in how the spell behaves, no matter what her husband said."

"Her essence?"

"It's an echo of her energy and her personality. Her soul will have long since moved on to its reward."

Despite Blaze's claim that Brayton was always around, Honey found herself alone the next day when she exited her last class, or alone in terms of guardians. The hall was filled with her classmates all rushing to whatever it was they had planned for the rest of their Friday. It was the perfect opportunity to visit the library if she'd been able to. She sighed under her breath. There had to be another magical library somewhere. Maybe there was one downtown or maybe there was a way to look at magical texts online. That would be even better. She would ask Blaze.

The straps of her backpack tightened over her shoulders and she was abruptly pulled into a classroom.

She slipped her arms out of the straps and whirled, ready to defend herself. Her attacker backed away, her backpack held up like a shield between them and a pleading look on his face. She dropped her fists, but only a little.

"Damien?"

"Honey. Sorry. I don't mean you any harm. I only wanted to speak with you a moment, alone."

"What's this about?"

"I won't hurt you. I just need someone to talk to."

"And you chose me?"

"I don't know who else I *can* talk to."

Damien did smell of desperation, and sweat, but at least he didn't smell like that awful spell, not as bad as he had, anyway. She didn't feel comfortable standing in a room alone with him though.

"You're lucky you caught me after class. Let's go to the student union."

"Luck had nothing to do with it. My brother had your class schedule. I can't let him see me, or anyone else that might tell him I'm here."

Honey snatched her backpack out of his fingers and put another step between them. "Why does he have my schedule and why don't you want anyone to see you?"

Damien sighed. "I am supposed to be alpha when my dad steps down because I'm the oldest, but my brother worked on Dad until Dad finally caved and made it into a contest. Whichever of us finds and marries a girl who carries alpha genes first will become the next alpha. That's why I went after you last semester. You stood up to not only me and Deacon but Brayton as well. I thought that meant you carried alpha genes."

"Is that why Deacon is in my class? He thinks I carry alpha genes?"

"He's good at winning people over, given enough time. He probably thought it was a good opportunity to get close to you."

"He hasn't really approached me since the beginning of the semester."

"Because he found another way to become alpha. He's the one who took away my powers and had me bound so they wouldn't come back."

"What do you mean?"

Damien's face contorted into a snarl. "That backstabber gave me the watch. The witch the librarian directed me to just so happened to be the same witch my brother paid to spell me. She wanted me to pay to remove the spell."

"You didn't hurt her, did you?"

He snorted. "No."

From Damien's tone, she gathered it had, unfortunately, not been an option.

Honey had the fleeting thought that with his brains and ability to control himself, Deacon would make the better alpha, but he'd stolen powers from his own twin brother and hadn't seemed to care in the least when his brother was feeling bad because of it.

"What did your dad say?"

"I can't tell my dad. He'll congratulate Deacon for outsmarting me and declare Deacon the winner." Damien slammed his fist down on the nearest desk. "I was hoping you might know someone else I can talk to."

He was clearly desperate. She felt bad for him in spite of herself. "You could try the librarian again."

"No. She told me to never contact her again and that if I did she'd send me to another dimension where I'd never be heard from again."

"Really?"

"Don't sound so happy about it."

"I didn't know witches could do that. What about the Council?"

"I don't want them getting involved. This is an internal matter."

He didn't say it, but she knew what he was thinking. After the trouble he'd gotten into in December by trying to spell her, he'd probably lose all chance of being an alpha if he brought more negative attention to the pack. Bringing negative attention to the pack was one of the worse things you could do in Alpha Meyer's eyes. Alpha Meyer had been willing to let Zavier, his own nephew, die because of it.

"Deacon used magic to do it. Your dad punished you for trying to do the same thing to me. Won't he punish Deacon?"

"He didn't punish me for using magic. He punished me for getting caught."

"And you've caught Deacon."

Damien sighed, "Yeah, but it's only me. Dad is just as likely to congratulate him as be mad. In fact, he might order me to continue to wear the watch to keep Deacon strong."

There was no might about it. Alpha Meyer would definitely order something like that.

She pretended to think. "The spell takes your powers, gives them to Deacon, but also binds you so you can't use whatever power is left?"

230

"Yeah."

"If the spell takes away your powers, what's the point of binding them?" Honey mused.

"It makes Deacon look even stronger if I don't have any powers at all."

"Right, but if it took them, why bother binding you? You'd eventually have no powers anyway."

Damien shrugged. "Maybe it takes a while for it to take them all."

"I don't think so."

"What do you mean?" Damien asked.

She froze him and turned on her magical sight. His molecules looked fine, but when she looked deeper, a ribbon of shimmering power twisting around him between the molecules appeared. She stepped outside and pulled an air shield over her to block the smell of magic, then stepped back in the room. She could make the ribbon shift by spinning the molecules or pushing them, but it remained irritatingly solid. She unfroze Damien right before her thirty seconds was up.

"Well?" Damien asked.

"It didn't work."

"What?"

She shook her head. She'd forgotten they were in the middle of a conversation before she froze him. Stupid.

"Um, alpha powers. You use them up don't you? I mean, if you challenged another alpha and you were evenly matched, you wouldn't be able to blast each other indefinitely, right?"

"Right," he said with a frown, "but no one is ever that evenly matched."

"Yeah, but if you were, you'd both eventually get tired and have to rest, right."

"Sure. It's like a muscle. Eventually you have to put the weight down."

"And rest while you recover," she added with a nod. It was a decent analogy. "Which means you must continually be storing the energy to power that muscle, so even if the watch sucks some energy from you, you'll replenish it. I bet all you have to do is remove the binding part of the spell and stop wearing the watch."

"Do you know someone who can do it?" he asked hopefully.

"Maybe. Do you have the watch with you?"

"Yes." He pulled a long box from his pocket and offered it to her. "The witch said it had to be in contact with my skin to work. It should be safe in the box."

Honey switched to her other sight just to be sure before she took it. The box wasn't spelled. "I can show it to my friends and see what they say. What was the name of the witch who put the spell on it?"

"Gwendolyn."

"Okay. I'll see what I can do."

Something heavy hit her shoulder, knocking her sideways. A large body that she instantly knew by shape and smell was suddenly between her and Damien.

"What are you doing here?" Brayton growled.

Damien took a step back and raised his hands. "Calm down, pup. We were just talking."

"You have no right to talk to her. You shouldn't even be near her."

Honey put her hand on Brayton's upper arm. It looked like it was starting to swell from alpha power but it felt normal. "It's okay Brayton. He just wanted to ask me about the spell his brother put on him."

Brayton turned on her. "Why are you in a room alone with him? You should know better than that."

She dropped her hand. After so many hours in the gym with him, she considered Brayton a friend, but his protective alpha side could be really annoying. "He's not going to hurt me. He wants my help."

"You're not a witch. He should go to the Council."

"He will go if my friends can't help." She looked up at Damien. "I'll text you whatever I discover."

"Thanks Honey. I really appreciate your help and if you ever get tired of hanging around pups," his eyes flickered toward Brayton, then back to her. "Give me a call."

Did Damien seriously think she'd ever call him or was he just pushing Brayton's buttons? Probably the latter. "I'm only fifteen so I'm more of a pup than he is, but thanks."

Damien's mouth fell open. Honey winked at him like her dad-dad would have done, then turned her back on both of them and left the room.

Brayton caught up with her a few moments later. "Sorry I was late. I had to speak with my teacher. You okay?"

"I'm fine."

"You really shouldn't be…" he began.

"Brayton," she interrupted, "I know. I did not plan on talking with him, but I figured out why the Meyer boys are after me. Did you know Alpha Meyer is making Damien and Deacon compete to see who will be alpha when he retires? Whoever finds a wife with alpha genes will be the

233

next alpha. That's why they were so interested in me. They…"

"…think you have alpha genes," Brayton finished.

"Yeah."

"They're not wrong, I mean, your dad could have been an alpha and that's probably why Zavier is stronger than the twins, because his mom was an alpha's daughter."

"My aunt."

"Yeah."

Blaze turned out to be an exceptional friend. After supper, when they were back in their room getting ready for their separate Friday-night activities, Blaze handed her a chapter on Mr. Witthem which she'd copied from a Who's Who book on great spellcasters. According to that, he did have a grimoire but it was locked up at the National Council Library in Boston. Of his wife, the chapter only mentioned her name. Blaze also handed her two thinner books on curses, neither from the series she'd started.

"Wow, thanks!"

"Only you would be excited by a book called *Deadliest Curses in History,* but you're welcome. I just need them back before my last day, but I'm sure you'll be done with them by then."

"I will."

26

Honey

"All done?" Liam asked when Honey stepped out of the classroom.

"Yep, that was the last one."

"Feels good, doesn't it, to have your first year of college behind you?"

"Yes it does."

"Excited to go out tonight?"

"I am. It seems like forever since we went anywhere."

"It's only been a few months, but yeah, you're right."

"Are you bringing Charlize?" Honey asked.

"No. Her last final was on Tuesday and she's starting her summer job on Monday, so she wanted to get home."

The weather was a perfect 75 degrees Fahrenheit or 23.89 Celsius. She was trying to make herself bilingual on temperature because really, the Celsius system did make a lot more sense and she'd need it if she worked in a lab someday. Flowers and trees had exploded into bloom. Poor Walter sneezed at least ten times an hour. On average, it was twelve. She'd counted. He'd finished on

Tuesday too, but he'd stayed because the rest of them still had exams.

Liam escorted her to her dorm, then went to do his own packing. Her dorm was a madhouse. Although over half the girls in her dorm had already left, including Blaze, the other half were either in the process of moving out or packing. Parents and younger siblings loaded with belongings crowded the elevators and the stairs. Several of the older witches gave her nasty looks when she passed them, but Honey ignored them or smiled. Nothing more disconcerting than a grin when someone was hating on you.

Honey waved down the hall to her across-the-hall neighbor who was stepping into the elevator with a big bag of laundry and a pillow on her shoulder, then unlocked her door.

There was a smell in her room that didn't belong.

She tried to step away, but her limbs wouldn't work. Something latched around her arm and jerked her into the room so hard she nearly face-planted. She tried to freeze whoever it was, but they pushed the door shut behind her, unaffected. Honey couldn't willingly move anything, including her eyeballs, which meant she couldn't see who was in the room with her. All she could see were the bunk beds to her right and a dresser against the wall on her left and a gray stone sitting on the windowsill across the room in front of her. The stone was new.

She felt a sharp pain in her arm, then a burning like something was being injected. She froze that part of her arm. It stopped hurting. Did that mean it worked?

"There," a woman's voice said in her ear. The woman might have been rubbing Honey's arm where the shot had gone in, but her arm was numb, so she wasn't sure. "Don't worry, this won't kill you. I get more money if I bring you in alive."

Honey wanted to ask who wanted her and what the stuff in her arm was but she couldn't open her mouth. She needed to prioritize. First, she had to get whatever it was out of her arm, then figure out how to move.

"I was told it would take 1 to 5 minutes to work. I gave you a double dose, of course, since you are wolf."

Did that mean she didn't know she was also a witch?

"Now, as soon as it starts working, I'm going to stuff you in this large suitcase and we'll take a little drive."

That's what she thought. Honey concentrated on thawing her arm from the outside-in and pushing any fluid molecules out of the hole. After what felt like a minute, she felt something warm trickling toward her elbow. For all she knew it was just blood. She kept at it though, making sure the rest of her arm didn't unfreeze before she was done. It was getting hard to stand up straight, even though she was still locked into place by whatever spell was holding her. Some of whatever the woman had injected must have gotten past her freeze zone.

"You won't be needing this."

Although she tried her hardest to lock her arms against her side, Honey couldn't stop the woman from removing her backpack and tossing it on the floor. Nor could she keep her from checking her pockets, or her neck for a necklace. She was lucky she'd put her hair tie on the end of her braid today instead of around her wrist else the woman might have taken it, not that it was useful since the witches had clearly found her.

The woman put something around her wrists, then said, "There's five minutes. Let's see what happens when I release you."

She still couldn't properly see the woman. She'd stayed out of Honey's line of sight the entire time. Now the woman stepped forward and inched around a dresser like it was a tight squeeze, but there was nothing in front of it. She was young, in her early twenties perhaps, with jeans and a T-shirt and a ponytail. She could easily pass for a college student. Maybe she was one. The woman stretched forward in front of the window and reached for the stone Honey had noticed. Something shiny fell out of the woman's shirt. Not just shiny, magical. It was powerful enough that Honey could see the colors between the molecules without consciously focusing. The woman tucked the necklace back inside her shirt automatically, like she'd done it many times before, while turning toward Honey with the stone still pointed in her direction.

"It's a freeze stone, in case you were wondering. It doesn't actually freeze you, of course. Your heart is still pumping and you can still hear and see me, you just can't move. I don't really need it. I can control you with a thought, but it's easier this way. Now, I'm going to cover the stone and see what happens."

She held the stone up over a little black bag. Honey lunged for her the moment she dropped it, but nothing happened.

She grinned. "See, told you I don't need the stone. You're under my power now. Into the suitcase you go."

A strong smell of metal and sweaty leather filled Honey's nostrils. She tried hard not to move, but it was as if huge cuffs had been place over her limbs. She couldn't

238

control them at all. The woman forced her to step into a large suitcase she had open on the floor. Whatever she had drugged her with was making everything hazy and her thoughts slow. It wasn't until Honey was lying down that she realized she should be using her magic and not her muscles. The woman's controlling cuffs were made of molecules. Honey concentrated on her arm and pushed all the molecules away just as the woman leaned over her to close the suitcase. The necklace pendant hung down, shining with power and smelling of protection. That's why Honey couldn't freeze her back. She grabbed the pendant and jerked it as hard as she could, which wasn't that hard at all. Her limbs felt like they'd been deboned. Still, it was enough to make her kidnaper tumble down on top of her. Unfortunately, the woman scrambled back up before Honey could react and jerked the pendant from her hand. "Oh no you don't." She shoved her arm inside the suitcase. "I was hoping I wouldn't have to use this, but you've brought it on yourself."

She slapped something onto Honey's forehead. Dark tendrils curled around the edges of her vision, then she was running into the burning house to rescue her mom. She was too late.

Notes from the Author

Want more of Honey's antics? You're in luck. It took me seven books to tell the whole story. They're already written and nearly ready to be published so if they aren't online yet, they should be shortly.

Reader feedback is very much appreciated. Please leave a review if you liked the story and tell your friends and your librarian. (That's me marketing. Impressive, right?)

You may have noticed the 'Clean Fiction' logo at the beginning of the book. I love to read but sometimes, okay often, find myself in the middle of a good story and abruptly I'm in someone's bedroom getting a play-by-play. Sex happens but I don't need to be there. I'm not the only one who feels this way. I discovered whole communities on social sites and a magazine devoted to clean reads. To make it easier for like-minded people to find clean books and to encourage other authors to go clean, I thought a logo on said books would be helpful. So, if you are a writer or know one and would like a copy of the logo, drop me a line. LisaL.author@gmail.com. I'd be glad to share. I have both gold-foil and black-ink versions.